I0541194

The Rise of Shams

a novel by
Soroosh Shahrivar

Published by **Morra Publishing**, a division of Morra Capital Limited
No. 6, 3rd Floor
Qwomar Trading Building Road Tower
Tortola, British Virgin Islands

www.theriseofshams.com

ISBN (paperback): 978-0-9932798-0-5
ISBN (ebook): 978-0-9932798-3-6

Cover design by Mehdi Saeedi
Book cover by Farhan Ihsan

For Massy and Sara

CONTENTS

Epigraph

"Light will someday split you open"
Hafez

1

Chapter 1
A Soul Dwindles at Dusk

Inhale.

Pilgrims from all over the world were making their way to the place deemed the pearl of the Middle East. The city was reminiscent of a modern-day Persepolis. Its buildings, like towering pillars, tested the sky's limit. The evenly paved roads belched with the smell of new tarmac, as if a million masons woke up every morning and by hand lay asphalt one grain at a time. People of all colors, ethnicities, creed and social statuses came bearing money, knowledge or experience in order to build their legacies in the new kingdom, sprouting out of the desert.

Dubai had arrived.

Winning Expo 2020 marked the city's coronation and the world could no longer deny Dubai its rightful status as one of the era's more illustrious cities. The people who flocked there were looking for some sort of magic to occur in their lives, and life on the beach under these concrete gazebos offered many blessings. Some found riches. Some found religion. Some found love. And some, most importantly of all, found themselves.

Hundreds of years from its birth, scholars from all over the world would continue to study this city where one man's vision and one nation's support built an oasis of fortune, wealth and hope in an environment with a climate so hostile that not much life survived it. It was an enchanted city, and proof that miracles could still happen.

But in an office that stretched an entire floor in one of the sky-preaching towers, the life of one twenty-six-year-old was about to come crashing down. His name was Darien, an Iranian who had lived his whole life in Dubai and had seen the city blossom into itself. It was a quarter past six and the sun was descending as he sat in his ash laden grey cubicle when Anju, the personal assistant to his boss, called him. She was a devout Hindu hailing from the rural villages of South India, who probably measured about five feet on a good day. A committed and selfless woman, she sent every Dirham she earned back home to her family working on the rugged, backbreaking rice fields of Kerala. She never romanticized her hardships but would bring it to everyone's attention at the office whenever she was asked to join the rest of the staff for their Friday brunches. Darien had always liked her. He felt she more than made up for her small size with her big heart and gleaming positive outlook on life. Not to mention he always would get a kick out of her thick Southern Indian accent.

"Darien, Mister Edward wants you in his office."

It was past the official end of the workday, but in the world of investment banking it did not matter how many hours you punched in. Darien took in a deep breath.

"Ok, I'll be there in a minute," he replied. The phone pressed on his ear felt cold, as did the entire office. He was born in December, and as a winter kid loved how the air conditioners in the office constantly winnowed on full blast.

Darien got to Edward's office, bringing the smell of coffee and cigarettes in with him. After cheeping a quick hello, he stood inside the door as idle as a statue. He looked down at his boss's desk. Rays of light from the sun departing outside the window reflected out of a crystal orb sitting on the desk, ricocheting and glistening right into Darien's clear blue eyes. He squinted and at that very moment he felt tinier and more insignificant than the dust gathering on the illuminating crystal bowl in front of him. He was zoning out and the voice airing from the Bloomberg market updates on the flat screen behind him seemed to echo further and further away with every passing heartbeat.

"Right," said Edward while brushing his pen across a stash of papers, his head and classic tapered hair down. "You probably have an idea why you are here."

His boss was an enforcing figure with a predator's mindset whose physical appearance alone encapsulated his persona. He regularly competed for triathlons and, aside from being strong and athletic, he stood at 6'4, which is why Anju always avoided standing next to him during the Christmas and Eid group photos. Edward Moroni the triathlete was also the Chief Executive Officer of the largest investment bank in the city. The simple yet ostentatious crystal orb was Moroni's prized possession. It was the embodiment of his life's accomplishments. Twenty-five years of work had led to the receipt of this award. A trophy endowed by a vainglorious enterprise celebrating men and women's futile attempts at conquering the world. The mahogany plaque under the globe read *'To Edward Moroni: CEO of the Year'*. And under it, *'in recognition of your leadership, vision and contribution to the regional capital markets.'* Darien was not surprised to see that the Financial Journal Institute had left out some of his CEO's more distinctive attributes. Such as his capricious management methods or his poorly articulated body language: a habit Moroni had of leaning sideways in his chair, which always left tiny creases on his perfectly tailor-made suits. And the one that Darien found most ridiculous and obnoxious was Moroni's tradition every now and then of sticking out his tongue, which was only displayed when he was more interested in what he had to say than in hearing anyone else speak.

"We need to have a chat Darien," said Moroni, his clean shave and chiseled jawbone still glued to his papers. Moroni wasted no time and got straight to the point. "There comes a time in a man's life where the buck stops but he should not."

Camouflaged behind his thick American accent was the "Cobra Hiss," a term spread by Darien and his peers through the gossipy financial district's grapevine. He had an oddly soft and mellow voice for an athletically active man with his size and stature. Add in the habitual tongue waving and the Cobra Hiss went synonymously with his venomous choice of words. Moroni was every employee's nightmare and he had quickly made a name for himself outside the company. A blunt and hardheaded boss who was as brutal with his own staff as he was with the company's competitors. A man not accustomed to the way of life in Dubai as he came from a faraway land renowned for holding the largest saltwater lake in the western hemisphere. Utah was a fitting place for him to have come from because his next few words were to turn out to be saline and bitter.

"Calling your performance and work ethic lackadaisical over the past few months would be holding it in high praise. You no longer fit well with our organization." He paused and looked up at Darien. "I am going to have to let you go," he bellowed out with his tongue on full display.

It was that simple for this coldblooded executive. Mercilessness was not a bad trait to have in the corporate universe. It was evident from the globe with the plaque, which was put there for everyone to applaud and admire. Darien lifted his eyes from the orb and looked right into Moroni's self-righteous face. A simple Trumpesque 'You're fired' would have sufficed. That his boss seemed to get a thrill out of his misery made his shoes sink deeper into the floor. This was not a chat as his boss so conveniently managed to put. This was an executive execution. Edward Moroni the Heartless had struck down what was left of Darien's career in one fell swoop.

Darien struggled now to break free from Moroni's reptilian glare. His first reaction was to tug on the bottom of his pepper-grey blazer, then to gently tuck in the side of his loose-fit shirt, which had run out of starch after its many trips to Al Nazeef Laundromat next to his apartment. He only had two white shirts left. The rest of his clothes no longer fit him. This was the result of a blemished diet that included late-night fast-food runs. He never used his yearly gym membership at Fitness First either, other than the first week after meeting Mariam, his now-estranged fiancé. He was adrift, lost in a world consumed by apathy. Four years prior when he joined the company, the young man was full of potential. How could have things gone so wrong? Graduating from Boston University and coming back to Dubai, he was the guy every girl wanted to be with and every guy wanted to be. A former standout soccer player, who was even asked to join the Iranian national team, now was a chain smoker who would end up breathing heavy whenever he went up a flight of stairs. A magna cum laude graduate who had been sought out by all the big companies but now struggled to show up at work on time. His aristocratic looks had matched his accolades and resume as well. Hair, hazel and rich in color. Skin so tanned after hours spent on the football pitch that it looked as though it had been dipped in a pool of ecru toner. His large penetrating eyes that had broken many a girls' heart. A nose and bone structure so perfect in ratio that even the finest Renaissance artists could not have sculpted it. The Darien standing in front of Moroni today was just a shade of his old self.

"Fine, I'll go pack my stuff," is all Darien could think to say. A part of him was enraged and wanted to react, after all the times Moroni had made senseless and politically incorrect remarks about the Middle Eastern diaspora. His favorite topics were disputes amongst Muslims, specifically the divide between Shia and Sunni.

But Darien knew that the only response to stupidity and ignorance was silence. He was rarely confrontational, especially when he knew he was at fault. He *had* been slacking off. Showing up late to work, not meeting sales targets and displaying no degree of enthusiasm at work could certainly be defined as 'not fitting within an organization.' He was not mad at Moroni; he was mad at himself. And that was it. Instead of retaliating with a flurry of harsh words, he was silent. He gave no excuse for his behavior, nor any response at all.

"I hope for your own sake, you figure things out and have better success in your next venture," Moroni said while the cufflinks, embroidered with his initials, rubbed against the leather handle of his chair.

Figure things out? What does that even mean? Darien thought to himself. For all of his career exploits, Moroni remained a tasteless man. He was not going to even bother imparting the young disenfranchised Darien with any words of wisdom on his last day. Nor would Moroni have the decency to stand up like a man to shake hands. When he didn't, in an odd way Darien was glad about it. Because if he would have, Darien's more sinister side would have probably wanted to break it off and slap him with it. He started to make his way back to his station, feeling as though he had two anvils hooked to his ankles. As he dragged his body along the parquet floors, he noticed each of his coworkers making obvious attempts to establish eye contact with him while he walked past. This walk of shame was nothing new. Many had been burned by Moroni, and Darien was now an official recipient of Baraka Capital's notorious dishonorable discharge. Everybody was waiting to see Darien flip. His predecessors always threw tantrums, scoffing at how lousy a place the office was on their way out. They figured Darien would be no different, and anticipated that eventually their piercing eyes would ignite the murmurs that would lead his serene demeanor to break out into a full blown cataclysmic eruption. But it was he who felt sorry for them, snug deep in their tiny burrows on the trading floor. To Darien, they were nothing more than modern day pagan worshippers. Congregants of a religion built on greed and hedonism. The trading floor served as their shrine; the phones as their Holy Grail; and the clients as the prophets who would entitle them to choose between putting the next down payment on a Lamborghini or a Mercedes. It was not losing the job that had beguiled Darien to this aloofness. He was mauled with despair because of how lost he felt.

With his mind so distant from the moment, he did not even realize that he had reached his desk. To his surprise, it was already cleared out. Clearly this had been a sting operation and Moroni had accomplices. His six monitors, one for each of the markets he traded on, were switched off. All of his belongings were stashed in a brown cardboard box. After four years what he had to call his own were a 'I Love Beirut' mug from Haifa, a high school friend whom he had promised a million times to visit but never did; a Mont Blanc pen, which Hamed—heir to a multibillion dollar empire and his first and, in his opinion, most honorable client—gave him back when the markets were booming; and a Moleskin notebook containing scribbles of a thousand variations of what would look like the sun to the untrained eye. They were doodles of the sun scattered all over the pages. He would always start his sketches with a circle only to be irritated and then cross it with a line right through their middle.

Darien thought of the little things he was going to miss. Like the daily morning coffee made by Jamal, the tea boy with a million dollar smile from Bangladesh. The firm saw no need to invest in fancy barista tools, so Jamal would brew good old instant Nescafe cocoa beans to perfection, adding a dash of thick Rainbow cream and a tiny drizzle of sugar. He was going to miss swiping his security pass every single day. The little white plastic card with a magnetic strip bore his name, photo and a massive lion's head. *Darien Shams. Senior Trader. Baraka Capital.* The lion logo made him feel empowered, like he was part of something much bigger than himself.

He was going to miss the screens scattered across the office and the frantic feed of live news updates on the global stock exchanges. Or the squawk box that vented out announcements on big market shifts. He was going to miss the stock market ticker that was plastered on top of the trading floor where his cubicle lay. Now all that would be left were his memories and what could have been had he been in control of his own destiny.

"*Salam* Darien," a voice interrupted his train of thought. It was Yasser, the stocky junior IT guy from Syria who loved clogging his arteries with snack bites as much as he loved clogging the company's portal with megabytes. To the rest of the traders, Yasser and the back office staff were errand boys, too low down the food chain to be taken seriously. They were regular victims of wise cracks and jokes for the amusement of those sitting around the bonfire of vanities.

"I'm sorry to hear you are leaving," he said as he fidgeted with his hands.

Darien was surprised to see Yasser acting uncomfortably. Although the other traders were ignorant of this, Darien knew that the young man had escaped a war-ravaged country against all odds, sacrificing everything he had built back home to seek refuge in Dubai for himself and his wife.

"I don't know how to say this, but I…"

"I know, you need to take my security pass," Darien interrupted Yasser, saving him from any more cordial discomfort. Perhaps the Syrian was sorry to see Darien go because he was the only guy from the trading floor who treated him with sincerity and respect. Darien took one last look at his name etched across the white plastic before reaching over to hand his security pass to Yasser. This was fate's hat trick.

He realized that this is the third time a life changing moment had percolated down to one single instant. The first was when a messy divorce at the age of eight left him as collateral damage. The whole saga came down to the day when he had his head resting on the passenger seat in the back of a white sedan. He could never remember the car's make or type. Throughout the years, he had erased the bitter memories of his younger years which were forced upon him and his older sister by his father. Their father, infuriated their mother's constant demand for a divorce, had decided to stage a family coup d'états. So one Tuesday morning, he came to school, picked Darien and his older sister Sara up and drove them off to the airport. En route to Tehran, where he was to spend his younger and formidable years, his father forbade his children to see or even talk to their own mother. They would end up moving from Tehran, to Istanbul, to Mumbai and then finally Moscow. Darien's father chose Moscow for two very simple reasons: an aspiring socialist, he had always dreamed of living in the Red State; and—the second reason being less ideological—he was infatuated with Russian women. He had made sure to share this last detail compulsively with his son and daughter when they were only children. Everything Darien learnt on how *not* to treat a woman were coincidental lessons from his father's promiscuous ways. Their mother very early on hired a private investigator to track them down, and began to devise a plan to reclaim her kids. But luck had it that their father met someone who would prove to be their unintended savior. Maria was a former aspiring model-turned-housewife, and, little did their father know, she was also a rattlesnake waiting for her opportunity to strike venom into an already poisonous relationship. When they married, he decided to start fresh with a new family. This made his older kids redundant, and he no longer needed to hurt his first wife by holding her kids hostage. He finally let them go after four years, leaving their mother to pick up all the emotional and mental pieces he had shattered for his own children.

They were rough times, and Darien had never found a way to accept the emotional blackmail his father put him and his sister through. Those years were all distilled in a single memory of being an eight-year-old boy, his head resting on his father's car seat as they drove to the airport, knowing a change was about to take place in his life.

The second incident was when he was sixteen. He remembered sitting in the locker room and staring at his jersey long after his teammates had all left. He had missed what would have been the game-tying goal in the biggest soccer match of his life. It was the first time in thirty-five years, since the high school's inception, that his team had made it to the national finals. With a chance for gold and glory hinging on his legs, he had failed to deliver. To that day, he remembered the feeling of failure as he felt with his head wrapped around a soaking wet towel in a dark corner of their locker room.

"There you go Yasser," he said now as he handed the security pass over to him.

He then lifted his box and headed over to the elevator. He looked into his reflection against the steel doors before they opened, signaling that his time at Baraka Capital had come to an uncelebrated end.

He got in with hands full and pressed the Ground Floor button with his right elbow.

He had hit the bottom. Now alone, he let out a loud sigh. But out of shape, out of mind, and out of breath—that was all that was left in him.

Chapter 2
The Turning Days

The sound of sirens filled his apartment's acoustics long
after the sun had waken, a gruesome ballad orchestrated by
his time-keeper. It was way past the 8:00 am alarm Darien
had set on the modern-day gnomon of his iPhone, which
had been ringing incessantly for the past few hours but
was still unable to wake him up.

There was nothing waiting for him to attend to and
he had found sleep to be his only solace since being fired
from Baraka Capital four weeks prior. Darien had not been
to Al Jebel Tower in the Financial District since. The
perpetually symmetrical tower was an architectural marvel.
So was the rest of the city Darien lived in. Dubai, with all
of its glitz and glamour rose in the heart of the desert. The
city was a Garden of Eden, a pristine beauty precipitating
with a range of ethnicities. The city defied the law of
nature and metamorphosed from an arid land to one with
towering trees and buildings scattered all over the city. It
was in this burgeoning metropolis that Al Jebel stood
tallest. Measuring in only at fifty one floors, Al Jebel
Tower where he had worked was not the tallest tower, but

it made up for what it lacked in height with prestige and a reputation as the most exclusive commercial tower in all of the Middle East. The twelve-year-old tower was also the most resilient of towers in the city's skyline. On its sixth birthday, the tower almost burnt to the ground. The incident made global headlines, featured ahead of more devastating news: racially motivated attacks in France, a hurricane of Biblical proportions in Thailand and civil war massacres in Syria. Cynics from across God's green earth wanted to see the thorns on the cosmopolitan rose that grew in the desert. They yearned to spot flaws in what seemed perfect, so as to make sense out of imperfections in their own personal lives. People needed proof that Utopia was nothing more than a theory, an illusion read in fictional stories.

But the burning failed to satisfy the critics, and the Phoenix that rose from its ashes shone brighter than the sun herself. The engineered steel trusses supporting the rebuilt structure were sturdy and strong. Strong enough to hold panoramic glasses all the way around from the first floor to the top. The pieces were so large that they could not be cut in standard factories. Engineers had to lay them out on a field the size of five football fields and cut them using special machinery. The panoramic glass pieces were so well adjoined that they captured the sun's pure reflection in a flawless mirror. Bystanders at the bottom of Al Jebel could bask under two glimmering suns. The owner of Al Jebel, a low key businessman from Ras Al Khaimah, had a team of hundreds of dedicated workers to thank for this soaring wonder.

But this is Dubai for you; somehow the most unreal ideas seem to come to life.

The majestic building served as a shrine to the masters of the universe: the movers and shakers of the banking world. At any time during the day, you could spot *Chartered Financial Angels* sitting in the park outside its entrance. The dome-shaped park, flushed with elegant flowers, had enough seats along its circumference to keep the smokers and coffee addicts content. They were what Darien used to be not long ago, corporate kings adorned in fitted suits with golden cufflinks, colorful ties, and polished shoes. The topic of discussion in the park always revolved around *sheep*, their term for high-net-worth clients, and how they steered them across lavish plains of green money. These young shepherds were Moroni's in the making.

Darien missed his weekly routine: getting up, putting on his finest suit and heading towards Al Jebel. The best part of his day was arriving at the park and seeing the sun wondrously gloat over how immaculate she looked through the mirror that was the building. He thrived under the sun, and loved to look up on his way to work and see its alluring mirage.

He so loved the incandescent glow of the sun that he never wore sunglasses, and believed that he had a cosmic connection with the star the earth orbited around. In his mind, there was a metaphysical bond between them. Why else would his last name be Shams, which in Arabic translated to sun? When he was younger, he would always ask his late grandfather why they bore an Arabic last name, even though their bloodline was as Persian as big furry cats, carpets, or pistachios. His grandfather loved telling him the story of their roots. He would always take him on a drive in his old Land Rover to the ice cream parlor and tell him how his great-grandfather, Amir ibn Ali, was a spiritual man—a Sufi of some sort. Having been born in Ardabil—a city in northwestern Iran, which in Zoroastrian meant holy place—was serendipitous as Amir ibn Ali also came to deliver the Friday prayers sermon. He was known as an introverted man who committed his whole life to reading religious texts. Then one day, he disappeared. Rumor had it that one night after staying until late in the mosque, he got up and headed for no reason towards Mount Sabalan, the same stratovolcano Zarathustra spent years meditating in. He was never seen or heard from again, leaving Darien's grandfather Jahangir to take care of his mother and six siblings. The people of Iran were by nature superstitious, their culture being woven of folklore, fantasy and mysticism. So the people in Jahangir's neighborhood were quick to claim the disappeared Amir ibn Ali as Shams-e Ardabil. Giving him the title of the Sun of Ardabil was their way of paying homage and respect to the many years he led their Friday prayers. They concocted this whole story that he had a spiritual cause that took precedence over his own family. Darien always thought it was their way of pitying the family and not ruining the Friday sermon cleric's name. Not long after, Darien's grandfather turned sixteen and moved to the capital in search of a better life for himself and his family. In order to move to Tehran, he needed to get a national ID card.

When he was asked what his last name was, the word Shams sprung out of his mouth. It stuck, and now the name was as much a part of Darien as his own limbs.

On this morning though, with his alarm heaving the sound of digital fingernails scratching across a board, he did not want to get out of bed even to admire the sun. He was too busy wallowing in self-pity and despair. Like an oscillating pendulum, every morning for the past twenty-eight days he had kept the same interminable rhythm. His aunt Roya would always tell him that habits took many shapes and forms. Whether good or bad, all humans have a predisposition to follow patterns. His aunt, although very bubbly and social, was a complete academic geek. She was part of the team that worked on the genome project in London, and her words of wisdom always derived from the Darwinian school of thought. She would always say, "Darien joon," *joon* being a term of endearment in Farsi meaning darling, "We are nothing more than a dot amongst the billions of organisms on the Hillis plot. You choose what habits you develop in order to evolve."

Darien could hear his aunt's words echo behind the deafening alarm. Though now more than ever was he the very definition of the superfluous man, he knew he needed to get up. Like a loris spotting a leopard, he slowly reached out for his phone and turned it off. A cup of caffeine might inject him with the impetus he so desperately needed to get out of bed. How much he missed Jamal's morning brews.

He felt haunted, sensing there was an inner demon that had been thriving inside his mind for the past twenty-eight days. This malignant, slothful, spiteful spirit was now so embedded in his DNA that he could not escape it, even in his sleep. He had reoccurring dreams every night about mundane moments from uneventful days, like when he would feel the sole of his leather shoes and the woolen fibers rub against his feet on a march towards his desk at the office. Or when he would drive down Sheikh Zayed Road in his rustic Range Rover and watch the banner ads hooked to the lamp posts flicker past, a series of soulless renditions of shoes, phones and clothes attempting to deceive him into thinking he needs these things. The dreams were an endless string of insignificant moments that made it seem as if he was never truly asleep or awake. This was so far from the destiny he had believed was ordained for him growing up.

Most five-year-olds, when asked what they would like to become when they grow up, are quick to say things like policemen or princesses or doctors or presidents or lawyers.

But Darien had not been like the other kids. He had thought himself a messiah, a savior, a Mahdi of some sorts put on earth for a higher purpose. Playing with others, he had liked doing what most five year olds liked doing in the eighties: collecting action figurines of GI Joes and Teenage Mutant Ninja Turtles, swinging off of monkey bars at the playground. But when alone, he would be consumed by messianic thoughts.

He once confessed to his mother that he thought God had sent him to lead people. She did not pay much attention to it. This was the same boy who would sneak into the kitchen, grab slices of salami from the fridge and lay them all over the house in order to make pretend that he was an apex predator waiting to pounce on and savagely devour his prey. So his mother allowed him to run wild with his imagination and never took it as some sort of divine omen.

Now Darien was mesmerized that the clinical term "messiah complex" was so accurate. His case had been nothing more than narcissism fused with delusions of grandeur. Perhaps that explained why he fell so far off after he left university. Reality had struck him with the truth that he was no one special. He was just a fool stuck in an illusory fantasy where the boundaries of space and time crossed over, lost in the prism known as the theory of relativity. His last name made more sense in the English language: sham, as he was something he purported not to be. He was a hoax climbing the Penrose Stairs, a never ending staircase that had no beginning, and no end.

He was no savior. Just a kid with a messiah complex.

He needed to get up. It was almost one in the afternoon. Another day in chronometric captivity. He was going to hope that Day Twenty-Nine will have a different outcome. Right now, though, he was going to pull the sheets over his head and try to escape the nightmare that had become his days passing by.

Chapter 3
The Dream

His eyes started to burn with sweat. He wiped at his forehead as he tried to catch his breath. He could feel his heart pounding out of his chest as he sprinted. He had reached the end of Al Maktoum Bridge, the oldest in the city, that connected the new Dubai to the old town and was filled with the smell of fresh fish and aquatic life. He had no idea what he was running from.

On the other side of the Creek, the old town was reminiscent of a huge bazaar, a microcosmic portrait of Middle Eastern life hundreds of years ago. There were stores with the most beautiful carpets, bountiful in shape and color. Herbs and spices from the furthest points of India to the lush plains of Andalusia were found in brown straw sacks outside the businesses that cramped up the alleyways. Their aroma bound effortlessly in the air with sound waves, comingling with the contour that resonated from the tradesmen's voices. In the densely packed streets, the shoulders of men who spoke Hindi, Urdu, Swahili, Arabic and Farsi alike glanced off one another.

Darien felt his thigh muscles tighten up but he still

could not stop running. He caught a glimpse of the Deira Clocktower about a hundred yards away. His breathing stifled the sound of engine pistons, screeching brakes and honking, but the bridge and the street leading to the clock roundabout were deserted. Not a single automobile was on sight. Nor was there a single soul as he picked up pace dashing towards the monument heralded as the oldest roundabout in the city. At its center four angled pillars came together into a hollow white pyramid. Spawning out of its center, at the apex of four arms branching off the pillars, sat a large white cube plastered with four mechanical clock replicas.

He reached the bottom of one of the pillars and took a moment to catch his breath, planting his hands on his knees with his head facing the ground. He was unable to notice the missing buildings around the Clocktower. Before his lungs could recuperate, a whisper broke free from the orbiting clocks above. He looked up, trying to see what it was.

Syoshant.

The voice whistled on. He squinted, trying concentrate on figuring out the voice's gender.

Syoshant.

It echoed across the air again. Darien had no idea what *Syoshant* meant, but sheer curiosity drove him to impulsively leap onto one leg of the pyramid in front of him. With quick thrusts, he climbed towards the perfectly situated cube. The voice seemed to be coming from inside. He had never been this close to the clocks in the center of pyramid, and now he could see how immaculate they really were. Gold stitched around the numbers gave it a blazing radiance. The short, thick hour hand, currently reading one, was filled with small flaming rubies. The longer, slimmer minute hand, currently next to six, was adorned with lucid blue topaz crystallites. The seconds hand was stuck on eighteen, even though it sounded like it ticked. Darien pulled his weight back like a stone resting on a sling shot, ready to lunge onto the cube.

Syoshant.

Hearing the sound again, he spotted a doorknob besides one of the clocks. He then sprung right onto the ledge of the cube, barely missing his mark. Standing sixty-six feet up in the air, he reached for the doorknob whilst balancing himself by holding onto the side of the minute hand. As he rotated the knob, a bright flash of light blistered through. The glittering light forced Darien to use his other forearm as a shield for his eyes, and he almost lost his grip on the clock hand as a wave of heat struck him. Darien unleashed a series of hoots, like a provoked gorilla in a cage.

When he sensed that the light had started to dim, he brought down his forearm from his eyes. And was instantly stunned. No longer standing on the clock, his feet were sunk deep into what seemed like an endless shoreline. The golden sand glowed with sparkles that looked like millions of tiny light bulbs. The sea, sedated and tranquil, wore the shadow of an illuminating figure hovering over it. Rubbing his eyes, Darien was taken aback to find that the figure emerging from a blurry cloud was actually a man covered in a long white cloak. His long blonde hair, matching his gilded belt, effervescently floated on air. His eyes beamed like two large green emeralds. An array of colors fusing in red, green, yellow and blue engulfed the space around the floating deity. Darien though could not take his eyes off the silhouette stitched on the chest of the man's cloak. It looked like thirteen equally geometric circles—six on the outer layer, five in the middle and one right in its center.

"Yes," the man gently said. He was looking straight into Darien's eyes.

"Who are you?" Darien said, taking a step back. He could have really done with a cigarette right about now.

"I am the name you heard that brought you through the cube," he said.

Dumbfounded, Darien spurted out once more the only words he could think of. "Who are you?"

Charmed by Darien's candor, Syoshant allowed himself a mild smile. "Who I am, or what I am, is of no importance. The message I carry is the only thing that matters."

The colors around him started to grow fainter as the shape on Syoshant's chest lit up, dazzling Darien with an incandescent golden glow.

"You, young Darien, have been summoned to lead a sacred crusade," he said as he glided inch by inch towards him.

Darien's mind went blank. He was mesmerized by the aureate plaque on Syoshant's chest, which was now less than a foot away from him.

Syoshant heaved a slow, meticulous breath at a

decimal only bats could hear. He said, "Forget every idea of right and wrong you have been taught. They are the reason your spirit has been imprisoned for so long. Should you accept the message I bear, then your empty heart and haunted mind will be set free and filled with the love of the Divine."

Syoshant paused for a second, it felt like eternity to Darien.

"When the time is right, you will need to follow the sun. She remains as your Golden Compass. She will lead you to the Golden Circle where reside those who bet their entire world that there is good in this universe and that God indeed is real."

"What do you mean?" Darien said.

"Just remember," Syoshant replied. "Follow the path drawn by the Sun."

Before Darien could say anything, Syoshant vanished, evaporating quicker than a shooting star in the sky.

Darien opened his eyes to find himself staring at the crystal chandelier he bought at a bargain from Dragon Mart, Dubai's version of Chinatown.

What a weird dream he thought to himself while he lay in his dark uninviting room. Darien habitually slept on his side with one hand under a pillow and his legs curled up, but was surprised to find himself now lying on his back. His older sister, Sara always used to say sleeping on one's back was much better for the body as it enabled better breathing.

Noticing that the sun was still not up, he lifted his head to get a clearer view of the analog clock on the wall.

The timepiece had been a birthday gift from Arian, his nineteen-year-old cousin in Tehran. It was plastered with pastoral steel and had the *Faravahar* hieroglyph sketched on it. This ancient pictogram was the symbol of a guardian angel. A remnant of a primeval daemon designed to protect the Persians. The clock's circumference was decorated with the flowers of life and in the middle there was a scripture written in cuneiform that read *Good Deeds, Good Thoughts & Good Words*.

The hour hand was pointing at five. He had not been up this early since the summer when every Friday he would go horseback riding out in the open desert next to Bab Al Shams, the five-star hotel that inexplicably bore his last name.

Darien wasted no time. He lifted his head from his feather stuffed pillow. The neurotransmitters linked to his muscles released a galvanic pulse all through his body as he plucked himself off the bed. He grimaced in pain. Yesterday was leg and shoulder day and he had really pushed his limits at the gym. In fact, his workout had been so intense that he had been too tired last night to change out of his favorite sleeveless now dry t-shirt. He still wore the rubricated crimson top with Che Guevara printed on the front. Under it, the now immortalized creed: *Hasta La Victoria Siempre!* Darien was no radical partisan, but like any good investing Samaritan he had bought the top from a street vendor in Koh Samui three years ago, when last on vacation.

He stretched both his arms and legs to release some of the muscle stiffness. Much to his delight, this morning he was able to beat the morning waltz his smartphone restlessly crowed every day. From the corner of his king-sized bed, he noticed a patch of LED light from the street lampposts weaseling its way through the slit between his maroon curtains. He planted his feet solidly on the cold marble floor. He had spent so many days in his room that he knew the exact layout and number of beige marble stones in his one-bedroom apartment. There were forty-four, one of which sported a small dent from when he had smashed his laptop on the floor the day he was fired.

Jitters overtook him. Either because of the chill travelling up his spine from the marbles or the lucid yet surreal dream he just woke up from. This was far from the mundane dreams he had been having the past few weeks. *Could it be because of the supplements?* he thought. It had only been two weeks since he started working out, after he had miraculously woke up from his slumber of desolation. He had also started taking supplements, a more than required dosage of whey proteins, creatine and Nitric Oxide boosters. NO, as 'broscientists' called it, was nothing more than a concentrated dose of caffeine, which gave the user a boost when working out. Darien had used NO to kick-start his healthy living regimen, and wondering now whether the dream was a result of the drug.

Now in the morning mist, Darien started to retrace the dream still fresh in his memory. Syoshant? Clocktower? Maktoum Bridge? The running?

Follow the sun?

He needed to call his mother. Interpreting dreams for Iranians was just as much a sacrament as reading coffee cups was for Turks. He was not superstitious, but considering how real the dream felt he figured he needed a second opinion. Since it was only quarter past five, though, he would have to wait to call her.

He got off his bed, still aching, and flipped the light switch. His room was a mess. Whatever the dream meant, it had given Darien a newfound zest to bring his life in order. And doing so started with cleaning up his place. He opened the double glazed aluminum window, his curtains greeting the incoming breeze by twirling like mad dervishes. Then a fly, seeing its opportunity, buzzed right into the room. After a few Fibonacci spirals, it landed right on one of the faded lotus patterns stitched on his curtain. Darien was mildly amused. The fly had mistaken the fabric for the real thing. Much like Darien had with his dream.

The room was a maze wrecked with debris. Scattered dirty clothes covered most of the tiles. A pile of dirty plates and fast food bags lay at the bottom of his bed. Worst of all were the ashtray and coffee mug, each with cigarette buds bulging out of it. The cup looked like a tiny, lethal bonsai cactus that should have had a toxic sticker glued to it. He looked around as tiny little black dots covered whatever his left eye laid on. These little black circular shapes were a result of him being a carrier of a parasite known as Toxoplasma gondii. People get the parasite by either eating infected meat or coming across cats. However, it was his mother who contracted it from playing with cats in her younger years and passed it to Darien at birth. Darien when diagnosed was fortunate as the parasite colonized right on his iris, but heavy treatment saved his eyesight beating the parasite back into dormancy. He had read up a lot on it. Both scientists and poets had written and studied this little organism that creeps up in human brains leading to a plethora of mental illnesses, the likes of neuroticism and schizophrenia, giving the carriers a high propensity towards depression and apathy.

He sometimes blamed his lack of motivation on his so-called illness, but it was the high degree of stigmatism and the black dots that always followed him which annoyed him most. This morning however he was not going to let anything get under his skin. He needed help cleaning up his dirty flat. That's where Lisa would come in. But for now, he had a few hours to start what he had been delaying for the past several weeks. He needed to polish his CV and start applying for jobs.

A new job meant a new start.

Chapter 4
The Call

Darien was wired in. He could not recollect the last time he had been so mindful. The dream was the elixir of light needed to break the twilight cast upon him.

He had managed to do everything he was supposed to do the past two months in one splendid morning: polish up his CV; make a short list of recruitment agencies in Dubai, London and New York; and a list of banks he could apply to directly. He now needed to draft a couple of generic cover letters to go with his finished CV, which sparkled with the profile of a trader with a Midas touch. His profit & loss sheets were proof that he was good at what he did when motivated. He never lost money for his clients.

His career narrative was beginning to sink in. He had gradually lost most of his clients, but only because herding his sheep to posh lounges and opulent restaurants, pretending to have a swanky good time, had disenfranchised him personally. His superiors had been irritated by his lack of salesmanship and what they deemed an absence of commitment, but for Darien it was that they had asked him to be nothing more than an enabler, a shaman helping the rich get richer, that he objected to. There was more to life. He didn't understand how men or women of his generation were demarcated by their vocation. How a person's wealth and self-worth were circumscribed by the amount of loot they made. That's why he hated when people asked *What do you do for a living?*

His transcendent sense of worth had risen and caught up to him. He did not like the world he lived in, and the people in it. He was just as much a victim as he was a culprit of the seven deadly sins. Greed, by which the world advocated and a career selected to serve his appetite for money. Pride, his virtuous vice, the voice that told him at a young age he was destined for prophetic greatness. Sloth, his abode to the law of attraction to just sit and all the wealth in the world will come. Gluttony, his habitual chain smoking, his indulgence of over drinking and eating junk until his belly would harden like the shell of a turtle. Lust, his karmic cheating ways finally catching up to him, when he himself was a recipient of its pain. Wrath, the world chewing and spitting him out just when he was beginning to question the present world's immoral doctrine.

And envy, envious of a time when the poet, the mystic, the scientist and the statesman were nobler than the merchant.

There was no need to leave clues on the many bleak and wretched hours he had spent engaging himself in philo-dialogue. He was now a member of Robin William's Dead Poet Society. And as the late great actor once said *Carpe Diem!* It was 9 am. Now would be a good time to shift into gear and do his round of calls.

"First, Lisa!" he said aloud, clapping his hands like a pair of cymbals leading a marching parade. Lisa was his cleaning lady from the City of Imus in the Philippines, a small city with over three hundred thousand citizens that had a city seal consisting of a church, school, road, lady, satellite and what appeared as the sun with nine rays. The sun symbolized the joyful, spirited and bright outlook of the people of Imus. And Lisa was the consummate ambassador of her tiny little city, which whose name in Tagalog meant a piece of land cut in the junction of two rivers. When her husband got a job with an Emirati freight company twenty years prior, his boss, a notable businessman, provided her sponsorship and allowed her to legally live in Dubai with her husband. With her legal status, she grew a business scrubbing floors, bathrooms and windows. She would show up wearing a large smile, with a bag in one hand and an umbrella in the other. The latter was to protect her dark complexion from the same light she embodied with her cheer, a light too plastered on the seal of the city she came from.

"Lisa! It's Darien!" he said, cradling the phone against one of his broad shoulders.

"My God! Sir Darien! How are you? How is your health?" She seemed just as ecstatic as he was.

"I'm good, how about you? How's work?"

"It is good sir. Too much busy. Too much work but I like it." Her loud laugh recoiled through the phone, and Darien could not help but laugh along with her.

"That's great!" he said. "I'm happy to hear that.

31

Listen, can you come to my place tomorrow morning?"

"Up course sir! I am too much missing your sense of humor!" She meant 'of course,' but it got lost in translation through her thick Tagalog accent. The response brought a smile to Darien's face.

There were flickers of moments like this one that illustrated the world still had some good under its crest of corruption, sin and destitution. Darien was a Middle Eastern upper-middle-class man who was on the path of self-actualization, Lisa a middle-aged lower-class woman on the path of survival. One stood on top of Maslow's mountain and was tumbling down, while the other was at the bottom trying to climb up. What brought them together was their love of a good laugh. She was not very tech savvy, so Darien had introduced her to the world of YouTube. When he came across a boisterous Pilipino boy who sang a song by Queen for a talent show, Lisa was the first person he showed it to. The kid was not the greatest singer, but he oozed with life and confidence.

"I want to break free," she had recited along with the song while laughing out hysterically.

Now Darien laughed and replied, "Great, I will show you some more this time! So I will see you tomorrow then."

"Great Sir, I will see you tomorrow!" She then stayed on the line, waiting for Darien to be the first to say goodbye and end the conversation.

This day was becoming better by the moment. The demon within was beginning to weaken. He jumped in the shower and cleaned up, finding a rubber band to tie his hair into a manbun once he had finished. The last haircut he got had been almost two years prior, but he was only newly on sabbatical. He no longer needed to don the Gordon Gekko look—at least not until the next job—and would let the hair naturally dry up. He put on a purple plaid polo shirt, navy blue pants and a brown pair of espadrilles before packing up his laptop.

Now ready to head out to one of the cafés on JBR, a road filled with retail outlets adjacent to the shoreline where a cluster of high-rises stood, he decided to have a cigarette to temporarily stall his exodus. There was an inner voice telling him that he did not need to leave his room, that he need not do anything but sit still and the answers he was searching for would eventually come. But he was quick to snap out of it. He knew better. Persistent action became practice, practice became habit, habit became ritual. The time was ripe for him to hone new rituals.

Instead of smearing himself with the stench of cigarette smoke, he grabbed one of his colognes and spritzed the air with the aromatics of ruby wood, pine essence that blended effortlessly with pinches of coffee and caramel. On his way out, he glanced at the only placard he kept, hanging next to his door. It was a collage of avatars that had left an impression on his heart and mind throughout the years. He was no art savant, but had taken the profile photos of twenty-five men, converted them into black and white and printed them on an A4 size paper. This photomontage—with copyright infringement written all over it—of immortalized men had no consistent theme whatsoever. He had a photo of George Soros pasted next to Karl Marx. A photo of Mandela next to Napoleon. The vibe was all over the place. Was he a leftist or conservative? Was he an activist or a pacifist?

It was not all black and white with Darien. The men he chose to emulate were about as different as day and night. He was Lenin in a Lamborghini. He was Gandhi with a gun. That's if any of those were to be reincarnated as him.

"Someday, my picture will be next to them," he whispered while standing straight in front of the placard. Was it fame? Was it power? Was it wealth he pursued? That was something Darien had locked deep in his own heart.

But this morning, his mind was right. He felt good in his fresh clothes. He picked up his iPod from the kitchen counter and headed out to the lift. He plugged the earphones in and pressed on shuffle. The first song to pop up was a track from Nasir Jones, better known by his pseudonym, Nas. He sang along with the chorus. *"If I ruled the world….Imagine that."* He must have heard this song a thousand times since he was in high school but the only words to the track he knew were the hook. To Darien some rappers were as much poets as Walt Whitman was, except the words didn't matter to him. He could feel the music through its rhythm. Give Van Gogh a pair of earphones and he will start bobbing his head.

He reached the ground floor of Orchard Tower. He had mortgaged an apartment there almost five years ago, but a three year delay had stalled the project. It was an ambitious undertaking. The building and its amenities were to run on an environmentally friendly ecosystem, but the engineering mastery of the initial developers did not foretell their poor money management. New investors had to be called in before the project could be completed. Darien's mother had warned him to go with one of the reliable developers or a group like the one that built Al Jebel Tower, but he was too entrenched in his own vanity. To own a flat in the only green building was, as a Corleone would say, an offer he could not refuse. The socially conscious girls loved the prestige and status of the building and would come over immediately whenever Darien invited them. Many of his concubines prior to meeting his former fiancé had come through the doors of Orchard Tower.

"Good morning sir." This was the building's doorman, Terrence, a young man from Congo who was one of Dubai's many working class denizens. A gradual shift in the city had seen fewer and fewer South Asian residents as a result of an influx of working class Africans.

"I'm very good, how are you?" Darien said while walking towards the exit door. It was a silly question to ask. He had the whole scoop on Terrence's life, and of course he could have been better. He was a hard worker who had left a tiny village in Congo to get a Bachelor's degree in pharmaceuticals from a decent university in South Africa. Unable to find work back home after graduation, he then decided to move to Dubai. The only job he was able to land was this one, meeting and greeting Orchard Tower's residents a hundred times a day. Here he was mourning over losing a job, Darien thought, while he could not even imagine what Terrence had to go through only to earn in a month what Darien would spend on a night out. The world had its prejudice: someone's misfortune served as a reminder to someone else of their fortunate life.

"I'm good sir." Terrence replied.

Darien always felt awkward engaging in small talk, so he smiled at Terrence out of courtesy and walked out of the glass panel doors that were made out of recycled glass bottles.

Stepping out of his conscious bricks and mortar, he walked down the road towards JBR. Under the blazing sun, his cool shadow dimmed the cobbled pedestrian walk. He got to the entrance of Café Milano and parked right at the table closest to a plug. Turning off his iPod, he unpacked his laptop and dialed his mother's number.

"Hello *joojoo*!" Massy Shahrivar said enthusiastically, her zeal a dead giveaway that she had been worrying anxiously for her only son.

"Hi *joojoo*," Darien replied. 'Joojoo' was a Farsi word used asexually to identify pullets and cockerels, but it was a family thing that Darien, his sister and mother addressed one another this way.

"How are you? How's the job search coming along?" she said, her tone as regal and strong as the sun shining over his head.

Fables are told of Old Persian generals who were female, conquering both land and men. It is rare to hear of women leading battalions today, let alone three thousand years ago, when the world looked at them as nothing more than caretakers. But Darien's mother was one of these generals reincarnated, a broad shouldered woman with hazel eyes and matching brown hair. She had a fair complexion as the result of the genes she inherited through her half-Russian mother, a super fit woman even at the age of seventy one. She was a strong, balanced woman who knew when to use her heart and when to use her mind. Darien felt she was the only person who understood him and his belief in a universal moral ground which was regularly broken instead of held by everyone whom he brought close in his own circle.

"I'm great. I'm feeling really good." He needed to put her at ease and let her know that he had been resurrected.

"That's great *eshgham*." Eshgham, a term of endearment meaning my love.

"I'm actually sitting in a café right now and about to begin applying to jobs. Weather's nice so I decided to come out and enjoy it while it lasts," he said. "By the way, I had the craziest dream last night."

After he had finished giving her a rundown of the rogue by the name of Syoshant who visited him, she let out a mild laugh of reassurance. "Hopefully it's a good sign. By the way, Howard is coming to town tomorrow," she added, bridging the conversation from fantasy to reality.

Howard was his stepfather's oldest friend. Their days stretched all the way back to their time at the Eton boarding school for boys, but they had chosen very different career paths. Howard was a former SAS officer who had been on missions in some of the most hostile places in the world; Gordon, Darien's stepfather, had dealt with some of the most hostile people in the world, notably bankers and lawyers from the Cayman Islands all the way to Japan. Gordon, who married Darien's mother a decade ago, was partially responsible for his stepson's career. It was Gordon who got him his gig at Baraka Capital by putting in a good word to the bank's previous CEO, Caleb de Morgan, who was a great guy and had really helped Darien come in to his own. They would always laugh about how he landed his job. When Darien had studied a year abroad in Edinburgh, he worked as a bartender at a place called The Three Sisters whose slogan was "Cause one is never enough." Caleb thought this was hilarious, and Gordon swore that he had been hired for it alone.

Gordon and Howard were a good example of Britain's posh and elite class; Gordon had an unusually great sense of humor—"A man equipped with a good sense of humor can get any woman he wants—just ask your mother!"—and Howard possessed an unusually great knack for storytelling. With these two Darien knew he was in for a stellar evening.

"That's awesome. I've got Lisa coming in tomorrow to clean my place, but I'll pop around the house in the evening then," he said as he looked down at the menu the waiter had brought over.

"By the way, have you heard from Sara?" Darien continued. "I have not heard from her since last week."

"I did, I got an email from her last night. She is now on the fifth leg of her trip. She sounded happy."

"I know: liberating, mystical and happy," he said. "That daughter of yours is like a human firebird, hopping from one mountain top the next."

Darien really missed his sister. Born in the same year, they shared a bond more special than any other pair of siblings he had met. They took pride in the fact that they were Irish twins. It had to do with the emotional stress and hardships their father put them through and how it differed so drastically from the binding love their mother had given them. Sara was everything to Darien—a mentor, a friend, a confidant, and a soul mate. The elder of the two, she had served as his emotional chaperone growing up, shielding him from emotional pain ever since kindergarten when he spilled a bowl of soup and she stood up for her brother when everyone laughed at him.

Most important of all, she was the Shams to his Rumi. She was his inspiration. Where he digressed after graduating, she flourished. After graduating from Harvard Law School, she went on to work for a couple of years at a prestigious law firm in New York. She then decided to move back to Dubai as she felt she needed to work for a cause with a bigger challenge. She worked for Dubai Holding, launching and managing their regional real estate portfolio. Throughout her stellar career, though, she still felt something was missing. Until nine months ago, when she just quit and decided to take a sabbatical. She became an astute yogi and spoke of enabling the forces behind her seven chakras. She decided to conquer the Seven Summits, the goal being to reach one mountaintop on each of the seven continents. She had six down, Aconcagua in the

Andes in Argentina, Mount McKinley in the Alaska Range in the United States, Mount Elbrus in the Caucasus Mountains of Russia, Kilimanjaro in Tanzania, Mount Vinson in Antarctica, Mount Kosciuszko in Australia and finally, the one that was left, Mount Everest. She had saved the best for last and combined she would have climbed over a hundred and thirty thousand feet against gravity's defiance.

"I'm glad she'll be coming home in a couple of months," he said. He had needed her more than ever over the past few months.

"Me too, I can't wait to hear all about her adventures" said Massy.

He then wrapped up the conversation by saying how much he loves her and will see her tomorrow for dinner. He proceeded on to handling the rest of his work, sending out emails to potential recruiters and companies. He asked the waiter to get him a cup of coffee to wash down the cigarettes he was about to chain smoke.

After about eight cigarettes and an hour into his morning, his phone rang. It was Samer, his closest friend from high school. Samer Saeed and Darien had spent their younger formidable years in the old part of the city in Deira. Growing up, they had shared many a night spent crammed up in one of the shisha cafes on Riqqa road. It was what the *cool kids* did in Dubai. Fortunately, their generation was not exposed to all the crack, heroin and cocaine that a lot of kids in other major cities were. Samer was originally from Iraq and Darien from Iran and, both having been born in the eighties, one would think these two would be sworn enemies. But as it turns out, they had a lot in common and formed a bind stronger than DNA. Both were stand out football players, both went off to the United States to study and both escorted more women in and out of revolving doors through the better part of the decade they had known one another. Now each had also been by the other's side through his growth into manhood. Darien was surprised to see that Samer was calling from his local Dubai number.

"You're back! How you doin', Princess?" said Darien in the most cliché Italian mob accent.

Samer emphatically laughed. "Now is that any way to talk to your father? How is my little boy doing?"

"I'm good. I'm good. I thought you weren't coming back for another three weeks?" Darien replied. Samer had finally finished his studies and now was a full-fledged MD with a specialization in neurosurgery.

"I wasn't chief, but what can I say, sometimes…" Samer paused. "Sometimes, life has other plans for us."

Spontaneity was something Samer was not known for, and this comment threw Darien off. His friend always knew what he wanted and planned accordingly.

"Ten years, Sam! Ten years you studied at Johns Hopkins and you still sound as corny as that snotty-nosed kid playing backyard football on Riqqa road!" Darien laughed into the phone, their insults being nothing more than their way of showing love.

"Well remember that girl I told you I met on my trip to London over the summer?" Samer said, his manner serious. "We've decided to get married."

Darien could not believe what he was hearing. He knew Samer had his head on straight. He always spoke about wanting to settle down once he had completed his bucket list by the age of thirty-five. Travel the world, build a hospital in Afghanistan, build his first home and then find a suitable candidate to settle down with. He had not scratched any of those off his list yet.

"Are you serious? You mean Aisha?" Darien had never met the girl but had had conversations with her over Skype a couple of times.

"Yeah bro, Aisha," Samer replied and Darien could sense the newfound ease and comfort in Samer's voice.

Startled, Darien reached for his pack of Davidoff Golds and plucked out a cancer stick. He lit it up and took in a deep drag, blowing the smoke up towards the sun. He spoke to Samer at least once a week, regularly messaging each other, and he would have expected his friend to have been more transparent earlier about taking such a big step.

"Wow, and you're telling me this now?"

"Man, it just happened. Last week, we went out to the movies and on our way back, I just had this impulse take over and I popped the Q. Fortunately she said yes!" replied Samer with enthusiasm.

Darien begun to tense up. His foot started to nervously tap under the table. "Are you out of your goddamn mind?" he shouted, unable to control his temper.

"What? What is wrong with you?" This did not seem to be what Samer was expecting from his best friend.

"What's wrong with me? What the hell is wrong with

you? You hardly know this broad and you're getting married?" shouted Darien.

"What's there to know? She's a good girl. She loves me. I love her. What else is there?"

"Sam, you know I love you, Bro, but you need to get your head checked cause you are out of your mind!" Darien said, throwing in a few F bombs just for good measure.

"I can't believe this! I knew you weren't in a good place, but boy you know how to drag others with you into the pit as well," replied Samer.

That was strike one. Darien was like a ticking bomb, and Samer had just opened a matter Darien had closed since the summer.

"What are you on about? I'm alright. I'm just not too sure you are," replied Darien sarcastically.

"Oh I definitely am. I don't think you've completely gotten over the whole Mariam saga, and you're taking it out on me," an agitated Samer replied.

That was strike two.

"I was over her before we even got engaged!" yelled Darien, taking even deeper drags from the lit Davidoff in his hand.

"Darien, I've known you for what, fifteen years? I know when you're lying. You know that's not true!"

"What are you on about? Why would I need to lie??" The passersby outside the café were beginning to take notice.

"Listen, Bro, you're just mad. I get it. I would be pissed if I found out my fiancé was cheating on me too."

Samer was clearly trying to keep his composure as he knew what Darien had gone through was not easy. But even though his tone was calm, his words were not.

"Man, as far as I'm concerned, I'm glad I found out when I did. Would've been a lot worse if we were already married." replied Darien.

He tried to ignore his own ego hidden beneath his words and thoughts. "And that's what I'm trying to tell you. You don't know anything about Aisha, what if she turns out to be an insecure tramp like Mariam?"

"First of all, it is my wife you are talking about." Samer had grown weary of walking on eggshells. It was time to set his friend straight. "She is no freaking tramp. Second of all, unlike you, I don't think the whole world is conspiring to get me. Not my fiancé, not my father, not my boss. Damn it, the world doesn't revolve around you Darien!"

That was strike three.

"You've got a lot of nerve judging me, Sam." Darien was beginning to heat like a cup in a microwave. "You seem to forget who you're talking to. I remember you bitching and nagging constantly over the past few years about how much of a mistake you made studying medicine. How you wish you had moved back home and were working. How you are miserable constantly studying and wouldn't mind letting loose every once in a while. Who was there for you? Who kept telling you to slog through it? Who was there when all your other friends vanished? And just because I've shared some of the shit I've been going through, you're now passing a moral indictment on me?"

"Darien, hold on a sec, you're reading too much into it."

By now it was too late, Darien heard his friend loud and clear.

"No, you know what. I'm happy for you. I really am. Do what feels right. But know that we're more evolved than apes, so don't take shit and throw it back at others. I gotta go. All the best with selling your soul."

"Wait Darien!" shouted Samer, but Darien had already shut the phone and turned it off.

His blood was boiling like the Dubai summer heat was coursing through his veins. He had not expected this from his friend. But more so, he had not thought it possible for anything to ruin his day. He retracted back into a comfortable place in his mind where he had dwelled for years, a dark and sinister corner. Samer had reminded him again of the drama he had to deal with at work with Moroni, that self-righteous hedonist who deserved to burn in Biblical flames. He reminded Darien of his father, which hurt the most of all. Wanting to fund a lavish wedding for Mariam's extravagant taste, he had gotten into a business deal with his father. And for the second time in his life, his own blood, his father, set him up and conned him out of the money he had invested in a real estate project. The man had given his first-born son an expensive life lesson: if your own blood will backstab you, a stranger is capable of the same if not worse. Still, he refused to let it faze him. Deep down in his heart he was still full of belief in a moral universe. It remained full of love.

And Mariam. Well that was a whole other story. A passive-aggressive Iranian who was taught by the best. Iranian mothers are bred as house wives. Although Mariam was brought up in Los Angeles, she was the disciple of a confused, manipulative and bitter Iranian mother who worried her daughter would go through life with the same lack of independence she had. And her mother trained her well alright. Mariam drew Darien into complete submission. Instead of encouraging him to fly, she cut off his wings, plucking feather by feather one day at a time. Through it all, Darien remained sincere in his love. He had not been loyal in his previous relationship, and did not want karma to come knocking on his door. So he kept a clean sheet and never cheated on her. Yet her occasionally raunchy behavior made him suspicious, and eventually learned that Mariam, who played the role of an innocent naïve little girl so well, was seeing a guy behind his back. Worst of all, it was her gym instructor. Only one of her friends knew that the guy was pumping more than dumbbells and weights.

It broke Darien to be once again betrayed by love itself. Love was supposed to be his escape from a torrid life. Love was supposed to be the easiest path to divinity. That is what Darien yearned for. But the deceit and lie which love bore crushed him. And it disgusted him that nobody understood that. Other than his sister, everyone only pitied him. It was the binding connection to a higher source that generated love. So when it ended, so did his belief in all that was good, pure and divine.

Darien packed his bag and headed back to his

apartment. No longer upbeat, he did not even look at Terrence before going up and locking the door on himself. His best friend had opened up bitter memories that he was trying to run away from, and this was the only place he could hide.

He was sitting on the edge of the sofa with hands dug deep into his temples when he turned his phone back on and it began emanating a green light, blinking like the eye on a lighthouse. Opening it, he saw an email from Monish. Everyone called him "Wolfy," as he had an uncanny resemblance to Hugh Jackman. Monish had a zest for life like no other. From motorcycle rides across Africa, to sleighing across Antarctica, to even sailing his catamaran from Miami to Dubai, he was like nobody else Darien knew. The name Monish gave his catamaran was Nirvana, a concept he embodied. He was the purest person Darien knew.

He was diving off the coast of Cartagena in Columbia, but, in some mysterious way, he was always there when Darien needed advice most.

Yo Darien!

I see what you're going through buddy. You have to stay nimble.

Have you ever seen a rhino lose it's cool when little birds pick bugs off its back?

Problems and negative thoughts are like those little birds. And you and your soul have to be bigger than that rhino. You can't get down over every poke that comes your way.

Remember it's the sun's heat and radiance that gives the desert dunes their glow.

It's really important to pay attention to the dialogue taking place in your mind. We are sometimes not aware of how self-destructive that dialogue can be. People get caught in a cycle of negativity and do not see how their thoughts affect their real life. They end up changing the externalities to fit their miserable way of thinking.

So listen and observe what's taking place inside your mind.

See how much of it is that evil destructive force and how much of it is a divine positive force that you can express through gratitude, hope, love and well-being. Negativity kills.

We've been out to the sea before. It's like the weed that gets caught in the motor engine. Don't let that happen.

Stay strong, free yourself from thoughts that shackle you and keep practicing the meditation I told you about.

I will call you when I'm back next month. Wish you could have made it. This place is surreal!

Definitely a place I will come visit again. Can't wait to be back and share stories with you!

M

This was Monish's response to Darien's incessant nagging about the things he was going through, and it was just what he needed. He sat silent for what felt like eternity and started to recite the meditation Monish had taught him. Monish had picked it up eight years earlier after he met a yogi in Goa.

Now he meditated every day.

Darien started to drift, the only sound in his room the oscillating of his own breathing. He roamed into a place where he was free of thought or feelings. He was present in the field of absence. He sat there, calm and quiet. His eyes started to get heavy. His shoulders started to loosen. His jaw relaxing more and more with every breath.

When he opened his eyes, he was calmer. He realized he had been out of order earlier with Samer, and reached for his phone. But his doorbell rang before he could call his friend.

"Yo! Open up!" It was Samer.

Darien ran to the door but momentarily stood in front of it to gather his thoughts and find the best way to apologize.

"Open up! I would've made it to Sharjah and back by now." Sharjah was a city adjacent to Dubai that had the worst rush hour traffic.

Darien smiled, opened the door and stood aside to let Samer in. "Listen Sam, I…"

"Don't sweat it, Bro. I was a bit off as well. When all is said and done, it wouldn't be much of a celebration without the best man."

Darien looked to the ground and was glad his friend didn't make it more complicated.

"So now," Samer said, wearing a devilish grin. "About my bachelor party."

ج

Chapter 5
The Wedding

He was still in bed at almost two in the afternoon on the Friday of the wedding. Samer's big day had arrived, but Darien was still out of a job. More than a month had passed since his revelation came in the form of a dream and the rejections were beginning to pile up. Darien had reverted back to being a hermit, bailing out regularly on friends, family and former work associates. If it wasn't for the gym he had in his building complex, he would have never left his flat. But he knew the "I have the flu" or "I pulled my back" were just not going to fly with Samer. There was no excuse he could make to get out of his best friend's wedding.

He was now convinced that the dream had been nothing more than a nightmare and what he saw nothing more than a nocturnal figment of his own imagination. The impetus he had gained from the whimsical seraph known as Syoshant had been short-lived, his supposed turning point nothing more than a cruel and sadistic hoax, and Darien was now in even more agony than before. He smelt a conspiracy against him that everyone in the whole world must be a part of. The euphoric feeling was momentary; it was nothing more than flares shooting off of a burning charcoal. They floated, illuminating his life and fizzling out leaving him in the same black pit he was in before.

Worst of all, the wedding was in Abu Dhabi, the capital of the United Arab Emirates, an hour and thirty minutes away from Dubai by car. That's where Samer's mother was from, and Samer and his soon-to-be-wife, Aisha, had decided to throw the wedding on the yacht of Samer's enigmatic father, Faisal Saeed. Darien loved Abu Dhabi's serenity, but hated the highway's tranquility. The highway slit in between two endless rows of thirsty trees and radars that stretched for kilometers on end. Since it was already late in the afternoon, he needed to get ready for the wretched drive.

He grabbed his tuxedo from the drawer and placed it on his bed. He had not worn it since Baraka Capital's ten year anniversary, which was three years ago. He lit up a cigarette, feeling miserable. He could not keep his back straight, slouching as though he bore the weight of ten sacks of saffron on his spine. With every drag, he felt his shoulders giving up on him as they slid down towards the ground.

He trudged into the kitchen to brew a cup of coffee so that it could wash down the venom in his lungs. While the water boiled in the kettle, he started to lay out his plan to weasel his way out of the wedding. He was in no social mood; what was he going to tell people?

"Hello my name is Darien" he said out loud, as

though holding a conversation with an invisible person.

"Oh Hello Darien, from who's side of the wedding are you?" he replied to himself with a squeaky voice.

"From the groom's side, we grew up together."

"That's wonderful, so what is it you do for a living?"

"Oh nothing really. I just got fired from my job because I'm incompetent. My fiancé ran off the treadmill with her trainer. And my father backstabbed me, digging me into a hole where I no longer have a penny to my name. Asides from that, I'm surrounded by pretentious crabs like you, and the rest of the world is completely falling apart." His hands swung from side to side as he set forth. "Other than that, I am great."

The kettle popped.

Samer's words kept echoing in the back of his mind, *don't quit on me, you need to be there on my big day!* He could not leave Samer after he had explicitly said he needed Darien there. He had promised his friend. So he showered, dressed quickly into his tuxedo and headed to the underground parking lot.

His car was as much of a mess as he was. His seven-year-old titanium gray Range Rover had never been the same after that freak accident the first year he bought it, and had only got worse as time went on. The car now had a problem which no garage could fix and Darien refused to take it back to the dealership because of the hefty amount they always charged. The car's steering wheel was so rigid that every time he drove it, he felt like he was rolling the car through a pit of mud. He had not bothered registering and insuring his car. By legal standards, he was driving it illegally. And he couldn't even find a decent and honorable mechanic. When he wedged his broken key into the ignition, he let out a *Bismillah* at the sound of it engaging. At least his car did not give out on him today.

After what felt to Darien like eternity, he reached the Abu Dhabi yacht club. A guard by the entrance was waving his magic red wand to usher the wedding guests through, where beyond, a barrage of colorful yachts and boats docked across the creek. They reflected beautifully off the shadows of the hollow water. It was a magical spectacle, almost as if painted with the brush of Monet himself. The yachts' berth was next to the Yas Marina Circuit, where Formula 1 would come into town once a year. At night, when the lights on its orbicular architecture switched on, the circuit would radiate like a constellation of stars. But Darien was too blind to all of this. He felt nauseated. As one of the valet attendants opened his car door with a smile, he grabbed his ticket and scanned the crowd for familiar faces. Darien was beginning to grind his teeth. He needed a cigarette. He wanted to crumble up at home and surf television channels.

The jetty leading to the wedding was grand. The sound of jazzy jingles aired from a hidden sound system. Women with gigantic heels, ornaments and gaudy dresses effortlessly floated on towards the yacht. The men, practically all in black and white, somehow complemented the contrasting and various dresses of the women. Everyone was here to pay homage. They were here to celebrate love. Darien by virtue didn't belong here.

The jetty led a narrow path up to the main reception

area, from where they would board Astana, the one hundred and forty-four-foot yacht Samer's dad bought and named after the capital of Kazakhstan following a series of successful business ventures there.

Darien could not find Samer. He was beginning to get nervous. He knew he would have to start mingling to fit in, but felt uncomfortable just looking at all of the wedding's guests. There were perhaps more than a hundred people standing around. He noticed a few of Samer's friends from college in one corner, but didn't bother going up to them. Although he had not had a drink in months, he just might need a few just to find someone to socially leech onto and get through the night.

He dredged his hands through his pockets, quickly pulling them out as the words of Mikhail, one of his larger-than-life clients from Moscow, came to mind. Mikhail had once grabbed Darien by his wrists and pulled them out of his pockets outside La Petite Maison, a posh restaurant in the financial district. "In Russia, we never do this!" he had told him. "We never do this. A man never sticks hands in pocket. What are you doing? Playing pocket billiards?" Now whenever he got socially uncomfortable and wanted to hide his hands in his pockets, Mikhail's words would freeze him up quicker than a Siberian winter.

As Darien contemplated this, nervously cracking his knuckles and fingers one by one, a guttural voice surprised him from behind.

"Darien, you are here!" It was Faisal, Samer's dad. Darien could tell how ecstatic he was that his oldest was getting married.

"Hello Mr. Faisal, I guess congratulations are in order. *Mabrook*!" Darien replied with the word meaning congratulations in Arabic. He mustered what little enthusiasm he had left and reached out to shake Faisal's hand.

"Congratulations? I thought I got rid of him," Faisal replied. Holding onto Darien's grip, he pulled him close. "But these two love birds are already talking about having kids! Now I have to worry about taking care of grandchildren," he said with a laugh. "*Yalla*, let's make our way to the boat," he laid his hand on Darien's shoulder; a fatherly gesture. An action so subtle yet it made Darien realize how he never knew what it feels like to have a strong and caring father.

"You drinking tonight?" Samer's dad was a great host, but he always liked to be one of the boys as well.

"No, I've actually quit. Besides I am going to be driving back." He actually could have left his car and carried through with the festivities, but Darien was in no drinking mood.

"That's great. I have some of my Russian guests here anyway, and you know how they like to drink." He was aware that Darien had lived for a few years in Moscow. "Also some of Sam's friends from America asked for it, so I have stacked it up in one of the cabinets below for you mischievous lot to have a good time—could not just leave it out in the open, you know, might offend some of our older traditional relatives." He gave Darien a smile and a wink.

Samer's dad had an innate ability to make people feel

comfortable. He was cool, a quality that explained his success in business. As one of the largest developers in Abu Dhabi, Faisal had a knack for connecting with anyone, irrespective of their creed, age or social status. He was a liberal and an open-minded man, one who wasn't a drinker but never objected to anyone who was.

"Alright son, if you need anything, you come to me," he said, switching to father mode. "I have to go and play the role of the groom's father! Have to go *mingle and jingle.*" A cliché phrase in English made almost humorous by the man's heavy Arabic accent.

Darien felt adrift on the Astana before it even set sail. After a few minutes, his phone went off. It was a WhatsApp message from Samer.

Don't be a prick and leave. Let me get through with everyone and we'll go chill with the boys and get the party started.

It seemed that Samer, the man of the hour, knew his friend too well. Darien, who had just been thinking of jumping ship, immediately felt guilty. It was only right that his designation as 'best man' obliged him to stay, even though Arabic weddings do not bear the tradition of a best man. He decided to slug it out and stay, but was so self-conscious that every time his glimpse connected with somebody else's he'd get distraught. He was sure that everybody around was judging and pitying him, so absorbed was he in his world of misery. He felt his misery was stitched on his own sleeve.

As the sun began to set, the yacht was on its way out of the harbor where today's itinerary involved staying out in the depths of the open water until the break of dawn.

The waiters and waitresses were threading their way in between the smiling and laughing guests. To Darien, they all looked like they were having a hell of a time. Seizing an opportunity, he tapped a waiter with his back to him on the shoulder. A drink would give him something to fidget with other than his hands. He grabbed a glass of pomegranate juice and immediately took a sip.

Cigarettes! Smoke! Darien thought to himself. This would be a perfect way to look busy. He migrated towards the tail of the yacht, an appropriate place to light up away from everyone. But no matter how far he retreated, he just could not get over the curse fate had cast on him. There was no escape from the pain and despair his life and loved ones had inflicted on him. Sitting right on the edge of the yacht, he placed his glass in between his legs and stared at it. Questions cluttered Darien's mind like a summer sandstorm: *What's wrong with the world? Why is everyone so selfish? How can everyone be so cruel? How can they be so heartless? Where did it all start to go so bad? When will things gets better? How will I survive tomorrow?*

His thoughts and the sound of the splashing waves were interrupted by a voice. "Hello son, can I join you."

Darien looked up at an old man, around seventy. Darien had spotted him earlier when they were getting on the yacht. He was the only man in the wedding who wore a *Kandora*, the traditional Arabic garment for men.

"Yes of course," Darien said as he jumped up out of respect for the older statesman.

"Thank you," he replied. He had a commanding voice, strong enough to muzzle the sound of the roaring engines behind them.

"So! What is your name?" the old man said. Having lived in the UAE for so many years, Darien recognized the old man's accent as Khaleeji.

"My name's Darien," he replied.

"Darien, Darien, Darien?" the old man said while he looked out across the water. "Are you Abdullah's son? One from America?"

Darien now knew who this old man was. He was Samer's grandfather from his mother's side. Abdullah was Samer's uncle, who Samer always spoke of as an amicable man. Abdullah who was Faisal's younger brother had had the misfortune of having a son, Khaled, who was quite a disengaged malcontent. He got in with the wrong crowd while studying at Miami University. Highlights from his four years there included drug addiction, rehab check-ins and the bearing of a child out of wedlock at the tender age of nineteen. Darien could understand why Abu Faris, as Samer called him, would mistake him for Khaled. His fair complexion, morose glare and morbid attitude must have made him a dead ringer.

"No, I am a friend of Samer's," Darien replied, refraining to use the word 'old.'

"Yes! I know you!" he said while letting out a loud gasp.

For a man his age, he had an unusually full set of teeth that shined brighter than pearls. Darien was drawn towards the old man's vivacity.

"You are his friend from Iran. The one with the Arabic last name." He paused to look at Darien, smiling almost as if he was recollecting his own life through him. "Yes. Yes. Yes. I hear of you. You and Samer were caught stealing."

Darien was surprised. That had been many years ago when they brewed with trouble as teenagers. They had thought it would be cool to sneak into the warehouses of one of the first of Dubai's malls and steal whatever they could get their hands on. The thrill of the act had been what drove them, and they had nothing to do with the few pairs of socks, shirts and trousers they stole which they ended up giving back. The rule of law in Dubai always bore mercy on those that did not commit heinous crimes. They had just got a slap on the hand and were asked not to do it again.

Darien was embarrassed, but Abu Faris just let out a loud laugh and said,

"Yes, people make mistake when young. I still make mistakes till this day." His last comment accompanied with a wink that wrinkled up the side of his face like the pages on a little book.

Darien laughed along and looked down at the bottom of his glass, which he had drank down to the last drop. He did not reach for a cigarette out of respect for Samer's grandfather.

Abu Faris then gazed across the seashore, his demeanor suddenly changed. Darien could tell from the way he squinted that this man had seen a lot. He would have really liked to know what was going through his mind.

Abu Faris was about to tell him. "You know. When I

59

was young, I had too much friends. Many friends from Iran. Now I do not know where they are."

Darien could tell there was a degree of remorse in his voice.

"When young, I pearl diving. In these waters, I dive with my friends from Bandar Abbas. We dive every day. Same thing. Old boat, wood boat, no engine, and no technology like this." He pointed at the engine rumbling below them. "You know Darien. The sea is, the sea is…" He paused, trying to find the right English word in his debilitated memory. "The sea is *Sahara*."

"Yes, magic" Darien translated. From the little Arabic he knew, he recognized that Sahara meant magic, charm, divine.

"Yes! Magic! I have seen many magic happen in this water." Abu Faris paused only to look down on his worn out but sturdy fingers. "I will tell you a story. One day, I was fifteen and I go diving with my father, uncle and weather was very cold. We go deep in the water, and I find a pearl. The pearl was golden." His eyes widened with excitement. "I did not understand, how pearl is gold? I show it to my father and he take it and drop it in the water. I say to my father, Why? He tell me, this water has Sahara, no I mean magic! And sometimes you leave things you find, good or bad."

Darien was immersed in Abu Faris' story, even more so in the enthusiasm with which he was delivering it. "Wow, how is that even possible?" Darien asked.

"How is any of this possible?" Abu Faris said while spreading his hands all around and pointing at their surroundings. He looked up into the dimly lit sky. "God works in mystery *Subhan'Allah!*"

An item as unique as a golden pearl was something Darien had never heard of. "That must have been worth a lot!"

"Of course!" Abu Faris replied with a boisterous laugh.

"Very interesting, how would you know where to pearl dive?" Darien said.

"This water speaks *ya* Darien. Not matter, Farsi, Arabic or Urdu. The sea, the wind, the temperature. Nature she speak only one language. We learn to listen," replied Abu Faris as he pointed his index finger to his ear behind his *Gutra* and *Agal*, the head gear Gulf nationals wear.

Darien went quiet as suddenly the permeating thrill Syoshant had given him in his dream rushed through his body again like shingles. He gazed into the eyes of the old man. He could not look away.

One of the waiters walked up to them. "Sir, ma'am asked me to request you join them on the deck," he said as he extended his hand to Abu Faris.

Abu Faris gently brushed his hand away, slowly getting up as Darien out of respect got up alongside him. "Thank you young man, God give me legs. I use them to walk. I come now." He grabbed Darien by the wrist. "Remember. There is magic in these waters."

And just as Syoshant had vanished, Abu Faris too turned and started to fade away step by step.

Darien was thrown deep into thought after the old

man's last word. Samer's grandfather had just hit the pulse Syoshant had, and he started to feel his blood course through his veins again. Maybe this wedding wouldn't be as terrible as he had thought. He decided to go back and mingle and jingle, as Samer's dad would say, with the rest of the wedding's invitees.

Returning to the front of the yacht, the party seemed to be in full swing. Some were dancing on deck. Others stood in pockets, engaged in scintillating conversations. Darien finally spotted the man of the hour and his bride-to-be with drinks in hand next to the henna table, which he thought was a nice touch. Since they had quite a few guests from abroad, they had brought a tattoo artist to adorn their guests with henna artwork. The mignonette tree that gave out the henna ink was a tradition dating back to ancient Egypt, and foreigners always loved its exoticism. Darien started to notice some of the women who already had temporary designs etched on their hands.

"Congratulations guys!" Darien opened his arms to give both Samer and Aisha a hug.

"Thank you!" they both replied.

Darien smiled. He could already picture them in matching cardigans.

"How are you getting along?" Samer said. This is what made him special. Even on his big day, Darien's friend was genuinely concerned about him.

"Good! Met your grandfather finally. The man is a walking legend. Insightful but really witty at the same time."

"Oh yeah, he is amazing," Samer said. "He is

hilarious. Did he crack any of his jokes?"

"No…" replied Darien.

"Well he came up to me and Aisha and looked right at her and said, 'If you like the foal, you will love the steed' and winked right at her!"

They all laughed. Darien was blending in.

"I didn't know what threw me off more, that my grandfather was hitting on my wife or that he knew the words 'foal' and 'steed!'" said Samer as he rubbed his trimmed beard.

"I guess humor has no age," Darien replied, raising an eyebrow.

"Look at you! All philosophical now!" Samer replied.

Abu Faris' words of wisdom must have rubbed off on Darien.

"We've got plans for you tonight buddy!" Samer continued, "Might have to take you downstairs and hit you with a few shots of truth serum, cause boy you're gonna need it!"

"What do you mean? Ready for what?" Darien asked.

"Oh! Remember I told you about my friend, Nadia?" Aisha finally interjected. "She's obviously here, so me and Sam thought you guys might hit it off."

"So yeah, you can chat her up with all of your philosophical jibber jabber," Samer added.

"Aisha!" Darien sighed. "I told you, honestly, I'm really not on that wavelength. I'm sure she's a great girl, but Sam knows, now is not the time for me." There was no need for him to open up about everything on such a glorious day.

"Time? When is it ever the right time? We didn't know..."

"Yeah yeah, you didn't know until it hit you one day after the movies. Your story is like a 'Friends' rerun man!" Darien finished the story Samer must have told a dozen times already.

"Darien, listen, I'm not just vouching for her 'cause she is my closest friend. She isn't like other girls. And I have a feeling you guys will really hit it off. Besides, she is drop dead gorgeous. Isn't that enough?" she laughed.

She didn't know that Darien had never really cared about girls' looks. He had had plenty of beautiful women during college. It was substance he was after, and that is something no plastic surgeon, fashion designer or gym trainer could give.

"I'm sure she is. But really, you guys will just make it awkward between us," he said.

"Oh no! We haven't told her anything," Aisha replied.

Darien knew enough to be fully wary of everything women said, even when it was with good intentions. Aisha's was probably an honest lie. "Ok, let's see how it goes," he said.

"Ok ok ok she is coming now!" Aisha excitedly pulled Samer's hand while widening her eyes meaningfully at Darien.

Taking the cue from her glance over his right shoulder, Darien turned his head to take a peek at the girl they were trying to match him with. Goosebumps immediately started to pop up on his forearms under his tux. Aisha was right. The girl was glorious.

Her indigo-smeared dress draped effortlessly over her figure, exposing her curves with every step she took. Her pitch-black hair perfectly straight as though brushed by the hand of Aphrodite herself. She had the deep bronze complexion of a copper statue. She was stunning. "Damn, Aisha. You weren't kidding," Darien gulped, hoping to slip in one more comment before the introduction.

Aisha smiled. As Nadia approached them, her poor acting begun. "Nadia, let me introduce you to Samer's oldest and closest friend." Aisha's emphasis on the words 'oldest' and 'closest' were a dead giveaway that she had already spoken about him.

To Darien, though, none of that mattered. He was completely smitten with this girl. She looked even more captivating up close than she had from a few feet away. She had an accentuated chin, with a Roman nose crowing down symmetrically from her eyebrows. Her face gleamed with confidence, ambition and dainty. Darien had never before known what motion seasickness felt like until the moment she looked right at him.

"Hi, Samer's oldest and closest friend," she said playfully while reaching her hand out to shake his.

"She is funny!" Samer laughed, broadcasting what Darien was already thinking. Samer thought he had noticed Darien, who had crushed the best of women in his past, becoming a bit tongue tied.

That wasn't it though. Darien was taking in heavy breaths only because he could not get enough of her smell. She blossomed with the natural fragrance of flowers that Darien was sure she must have been conceived under a magnolia tree. Under her own fragrance, his nostrils could pick up a slight hint of incense, or *oud* as it is known in the UAE. A beautiful diamond necklace resting on her décolletage was possibly the thurible that gave away this deific aroma. If he wanted to have any chance at this divine being, he would need to get his act together.

He fixed his posture, trying to act nonchalant, and stretched his hand towards her. "Darien, the name is Darien."

"Nice to meet you," she replied with her eyelashes flapping swifter than Darien's heartbeats.

"Pleasure is all mine," seemed like what James Bond would've said. He would need to play this smart. And playing hard to get would be smart. He cut the conversation short. "Well, I'm going to grab a drink. It was nice meeting you, Nadia. Guys, see you around!" Darien said to Samer and Aisha.

They both looked surprised, but Nadia didn't seem to mind any of it. She smiled at Darien and carried on talking to Aisha.

Darien made his way down to the cabinet where the drinks and rowdy twenty-year-olds were. They amused Darien. He had been one of them not long ago. He wanted to stay there just long enough to buy some time to draw up a strategy of how he would get Nadia to go on a date with him, but the next few hours passed by uneventfully. It was already past midnight, and the boat had anchored quite a while back, when he decided to head back up with no plan but hope for some miracle to happen.

The party was still going on full throttle. Iranians and

Arabs are alike when it comes to celebrating. They can go on from dusk till dawn. Darien saw Nadia right in the thick of the dance floor, spinning around, flaunting her mesmerizing smile, and allowing her hands to swim in an imaginary pool of bliss. Darien was not alone in being hypnotized by her snake charm. The men stood with jaws anchored to their chins and the women gripped their partners' hands tight so as not to lose out to the competition.

It was pointless. Darien wasn't going to jump in the middle and dance. He decided to go back to the tail of the yacht and have a cigarette. He headed out, took out his pack of Davidoff's and lit one cigarette up. Looking around, all he saw was darkness in contrast to the lights and music blasting behind him. He planted his hands on the ridge handle bars around the boat and carried on staring into the abyss.

"Mind if I join you?" a serenading voice interrupted him.

Darien knew instantly it was Nadia. He swept himself off the ledge. "Sure, all I've got are Golds." He could not think of anything better or more suave to say.

"What girl doesn't like gold?" she said, seeming to sense that he was a bit thrown off.

He handed her a cigarette and lit it for her. If he was going to be a prick, he might as well be a chivalrous prick.

Nadia took a deep drag and looked right into Darien's eyes. She held his gaze, making Darien feel a bit uneasy.

"So that was awkward!" she said, smoothly taking another drag.

"What was?" Darien had a hunch where she was going with this.

"The whole match-making thing," she replied.

Darien figured it would be pointless now to pretend they did not know what Sam and Aisha had planned. "Yeah it did throw me off a little bit as well," he said while scratching his perfectly tied hair.

"Aisha has been talking about you non-stop since she spoke to you on Skype months back."

Darien almost felt guilty. Here Aisha was putting in a good word for him while he just a few weeks back had been putting her dignity under the microscope and trying to break Sam and her up.

"Well they've both talked about you a lot as well," said Darien unconvincingly.

"Look I get it. You wanted to play your cards right so you thought the right thing was to give me the cold shoulder," she said as she took in another drag.

She clearly did not waste any time beating around the bush. This was new territory to Darien. He had never met a girl who shot an arrow straighter than Cupid did.

"What do you mean? I'm not sure I follow you." He was lying between his teeth.

"Really? You've been staring at me all night." She waited to hear what Darien had to say for himself.

"I have?" Darien started to relax. His playful nature was beginning to wake from its slumber.

"Yes, you have. And I know how you were, let's say, a bit bashful when I walked over as you were standing next to those cheeky monkeys." She was referring to the newlyweds.

It had been a very long time Darien had flirted with anyone, but this was his element, and now he was beginning to have fun. "My my, are we not full of ourselves?" he said.

"No, not full of myself, just confident," she replied. That word, confidence, was like butter on a hot stove for Darien, what he considered the most attractive quality in a woman.

"That you are indeed," Darien replied as he took in a deep drag and looked down on her ankles that lay confidently on top of her stilettos.

"And since you didn't bother coming up to me, I decided to follow you out here and spark up a conversation myself," she said as she crossed her hand across her chest, cigarette facing away from them.

"You know, I grew up in New York, but I am still Arabic. We like our men to be the first to make a move," she said, smiling a grin at Darien that he knew was the end of him.

It would be futile to attempt to outsmart this girl. Darien could tell she was no ordinary Gucci-slinging, Louboutin-trotting, Chanel-wearing girl. He needed to be sincere.

"You're right. And for that I apologize. How can I make it up to you?" he said as he smiled back.

"For starters, you can tell me when you can take me out for dinner," she said. This girl knew what she wanted and how to get it. By this point Darien was just putty in her hands.

"Consider it done, what else would you like?" he replied.

"What else? You're quite generous, I didn't have anything else in mind," she said, throwing her cigarette out in the water. "Well. There is one thing I wanted to do, but Aisha talked me out of it."

"What is it?" he replied eagerly.

"I've got this urge to go for a dip in the water, but Aisha said it's too dark and dangerous to jump out." She paused for him to gather his reaction.

This was his moment, he could really impress her if he made it happen. But clearer heads prevailed and he knew it would not be the smartest thing to do. "I really like your sense of adventure, but it's pitch black, not to mention we are pretty far off the coast. There could be sharks lurking under there." He pointed out at the water.

"I know! But I want to do something to remember this wedding by!"

"Isn't the fact that your best friend is getting married enough for you?" he said. Her last comment had taken him an inch back.

"Ah! You're right, better to just forget about it," she said.

As she idly worked to fix the side of her dress, Darien looked at her hand. And there it was. The henna painting she had in between her thumb and index finger.

"What is that?" Darien said in awe.

Nadia, startled by Darien's reaction, looked towards where he was pointing. "What? This? It is henna," she said.

"I know, but what is it supposed to be? The design I mean, what is that?" Darien came off as though he was interrogating her.

"Oh! It's the sun. Isn't it cute?"

Follow the sun

Darien went quiet. A force overtook him. The message Syoshant had delivered in his dream was staring right at him.

"You know what, Nadia. I say let's do it," he said with new vigor.

"Do what?" she replied. Now Nadia was confused.

"Let's jump in. I'll jump with you!" he said. He swayed from side to side, unable to hold his divine excitement back.

"Are you serious?"

"I am. Let's go for it right now!" His mind was racing. It seemed as though Syoshant's voice was coming from afar.

Follow the sun

"I hope this is not one of those 'Titanic'—you jump I jump—moments, cause I was just being a bit rebellious," she said, backing away slightly.

But she was too late, Darien now knew this was a premonition he could not walk away from. He also knew he could not share it with her for fear that Nadia might walk away. Guessing she was a bit of an adrenaline junkie, he insisted a few more times on why they should jump.

"Ok ok, this is so exciting!" Nadia couldn't hold her eagerness back after a few minutes. She took off her stilettos and reached for a pair of nearby life jackets.

Darien was not thinking clearly anymore. He took out his cell phone, wallet and keys and placed them on the floor. Any act of bravado would only impress this girl more. Before Nadia could turn, he dove head first into the shivering cold water with all of his clothes on.

"Are you crazy?" Nadia yelled out. She hadn't thought they were actually going through with it.

"The water is freaking freezing," he shouted back while paddling to stay afloat. "Are you coming in or what?"

Nadia now had half of her body over the ledge trying to get a better look at the one person on the boat who seemed more insane than she was. "Darien! I didn't mean like this! We should've told one of the skippers first!"

"Oh now you're just making excuses. Just dive in. Put the jacket on and dive in!" His lips were beginning to tremor. It was a winter's night and the water was as cold as a glass of ice.

"You are crazy, Darien."

It seemed to Darien that perhaps Nadia now couldn't help but be charmed by him, but the waves had started to pick up and he had to paddle now not only to stay warm but to stay afloat. The current became stronger with every passing second.

"Darien, it looks pretty tense out there. Come up. I don't think it's safe," Nadia said.

Darien was beginning to feel the pressure of the waves as his body swayed back and forth over what seemed like ten-foot waves.

Nadia threw in a lifebuoy and yelled, "Darien, grab on

please!"

Darien tried to swim towards the lifebuoy but the harder he swam the further away he got. Nadia started panicking and yelling for help, her voice receding with each current that hit him.

Breathe. Only breathe. He thought to himself. He helplessly waved his hands and legs, but the tide kept dragging him underwater. He could barely make out Nadia running inside to get help. There was not enough oxygen getting to his brain to even bring him to regret what a silly mistake he had made. He paddled harder. It was becoming more difficult to breathe, and the yacht now looked like nothing more than a star on the horizon.

His clothes began to feel heavy. His chest began to feel even heavier.

And before he knew it, he had blacked out.

ح

Chapter 6
The Awakening

In a state of semi-consciousness, he could feel the scorching sun on his skin. His chest cavity rose and fell gently. The water that charged him now came with grains of sand that like a thousand little ants nibbled on the side of his face. He could hear a voice hovering right above him as he struggled to stay conscious.

"Manibeb! Iyednez?"

He mustered just enough energy to unglue his eyelids. Everything was a blur. He could only make out the shape of what looked like a man fluttering above him. He let out a moan and tried to lift his head to get a better glimpse, but his eyes gave out on him. He passed out again.

What must have been only a few minutes later he gained his bearings back. The voice was still ranting on. It wasn't Arabic. Nor Farsi. Or any other language spoken on his side of the world. But he sure as fire had not drifted thousands of miles to some island off the coast of Africa, and he understood this peculiar dialect somehow. Could it be another dream?

The man bleated on and on, his voice beginning to

irritate Darien. His eardrums were beginning to oscillate like the many days his alarm would ring yet unable to wake him up. The voice was growing clearer and clearer, and as Darien opened his eyes, he yelled out, "Hera! Hera! Temavanahsim!"

Darien's eyes opened wide quicker than a flash goes off on a camera. *What in God's name did I just say?* But he knew the answer to his own question. His words had meant, "Yes! Yes! I hear you!" He jolted straight up, rubbing his wet sleeve over his face. He looked around in a daze, completely ignoring the man standing to his right.

"Rise and shine!" said the man.

Darien now realized his body was nearly submerged in sand. He started to comb his long wet hair to the side of his face to look at the man, and noticed a pair of cloven hooves standing beside him. Working his way up from the brown hooves, what he saw next threw him into a complete frenzy.

It was a goat. A big oversized goat with a human's face.

Horror consumed Darien. He jumped and started to backpedal into the water as he stared in awe at this ungodly animal.

"Relax Darien!" the thing said.

Stunned, Darien stopped moving away. "What? How do you know my name? What am I saying? What's coming out of my mouth? Who are you? What are you?"

"Look, you had a rough ride, I get it. Just take a deep breath and I will explain everything to you," the goat said.

Deep breaths. That's it! Deep breaths. This must be

nothing more than another lucid dream, Darien thought to himself. He had that one dream with Syoshant. This must be the same thing. How else would he be able to communicate with a goat with a man's face in a complete foreign language?

Darien had managed to crawl his way a few yards closer to the water. Still a bit drowsy, his legs were giving out from under him as he tried to get up. He was doing the chicken dance. The same dance boxers do when they get knocked out. His head was spinning. Seeing Darien in distress, the man with the goat's face started to walk towards him.

Before he could say anything, Darien shrieked, "Don't you take one more step." He then paused, "or whatever those are, don't you come closer!"

"This is just a dream. This is just a dream." Darien must have repeated that over a dozen times as he stood in the water, hair disheveled. His wet tuxedo was so heavy it was difficult to stand. He started to slap his own face, thinking it would help him wake up. "I must be asleep. I must be asleep. I need to wake up."

The creature in front of Darien raised an eyebrow. "Right, I think you've got it the other way around."

Darien turned to run deeper into the water, a knee-jerk reaction that got the creature riled up.

"Hold on, hold on Darien!"

Darien thrust his head into the water, hoping that drowning would wake him up. He could taste the saline water filling his lungs.

"Damn it! You're more stubborn than my furry

cousins," the creature yelled as he ran towards Darien. He yanked Darien out of the water and started to drag him by his collar back on shore.

"What is the matter with you? Do you not listen at all?" the creature said, seeming just as confused as Darien was. "You need to collect yourself!"

"What is going on? Where am I?" Darien coughed and spat as he tried to catch his breath.

Reality was beginning to sink in around him as his senses grew sharper. This was no dream. The drowning had felt real. The sand under his feet felt real. And in a peculiar way, this imaginary creature looked real.

"Is this a prank? Is Samer behind this?" His best friend had been pulling pranks since childhood, but he knew already that this was not the case. "Man did he go out of his way to get me. Is that a costume? Seriously, who are you?"

"Does it look like I'm wearing a costume?" the creature replied, stretching his arms out while looking seemingly a little irked. "The name is Kafka since you ask. And before you flip again, just give me a freaking moment to explain," he said.

Darien was having trouble coming to grips with what stood in front of him. Kafka had a strong build, even though it looked like he was a few inches shorter than Darien. His face was accentuated by a full beard below his flat nose and two tiny horns that arched over the crown of his head. He could spit words at an alarming fast rate.

"Before you have another tantrum, just look around you," Kafka said. "You, my good man, have reached that point where there is no more turning back."

Darien took a moment to take this in, the logical side of his brain rushing once more to his aid. This could very well be a research center and the goat, or Kafka as he called himself, a science experiment gone wrong. He knew Abu Dhabi was home to more than two hundred islands, and perhaps this was one of them which was kept under wraps for healthcare experimentation.

But it was not just Kafka that was out of place; the island in front of him looked like a place out of a fairytale. There were lush green bushes corroding like melted clocks on the sand. The island down shore was swimming in green vegetation with shades of color he had never seen before. Moisture rose from the plants, creating a thin hanging cloud over the island over an endless array of coves and tress scattered all around. And even though he was no botanical expert, he knew that this sort of plant life did not exist on the arid islands of the Middle East. The island's green horizon was surreal. It reminded Darien of the forests in the outskirts of Moscow. They were one of the very few good memories he had of his childhood there when his very own father kept him and his sister captive in the city.

"Well as much as I'd like to stand around and share this moment with you, I promised Evren I would take you back to him. So we best get a move on," Kafka said, breaking the serene silence that had hypnotized Darien.
"I am not even going to bother asking who Evren is," Darien murmured. He knew he was not going to get any rational explanation. He was in over his head.

"Great, then let's make a move!" Kafka replied as he turned and started to walk into the tropical jungle. "History begins in that moment of space and time when a traveler takes one step forward." He let out a loud laugh. "See, I pride myself in being something of a philosopher."

Darien just stared at him, following but also making sure he was a few steps behind so nothing else would catch him off guard. He noticed large boulders and lines of jagged cliffs flowing with beautifully arranged floral patterns. The deeper they walked into the forest the more he was amazed by what he saw. There was a range of deciduous trees, each glowing with effervescent light from the humidity given off. He was walking on flowering plants and shrubs so soft that he felt like he was walking on air.

The shrubs, brushes and trees were all tangled together creating a network of various shades of green mixed with a range of colors of the flowers on the ground. Even with all of the natural beauty that surrounded him, he kept on glancing every few seconds at Kafka. He walked like a human. And he sure spoke like one. But Darien just could not take his eyes off the man's horns and hooves. Kafka had noticed how Darien kept staring.

"I can't take this anymore!" he yelled as he turned to face Darien. "Get it out! Get it out of your system!"

"Look," Darien said as he leaned his weight on his right leg. "Bear in mind the current circumstances. I have just been washed ashore on an island, and the first thing I see is you." He needed to be as sensitive as possible so as not to anger the potentially dangerous mutated being. "So,

79

don't take it the wrong way when I ask you, what are you?"

"See, that wasn't that hard now was it? I am an Ashkhasi," Kafka said with fluid and calm conviction. "I come from Ashkhas Island. The same one you are standing on with that baffled grin," he continued as he pointed at Darien's face.

Darien was relieved to at least know the name of where he was. It still did not give any clues to where he was and who Kafka was.

"Look, I get it. I really do. You're confused, but you still are not asking me the right questions," Kafka said. "Listen, the old man Evren gave me strict orders not to ramble on as it might throw you off, so let's just keep moving and he will explain everything to you, how does that sound?"

Darien said out loud what was echoing in his mind. "Is this for real?"

"Sometimes what is real may not necessarily be real," Kafka stated matter-of-factly.

The goat wasn't kidding, Darien thought. He really was a philosophizing fuzz ball walking on two hooves. Kafka had a peaceful aura about him, even though he spoke fast and constantly waved his hands around. Darien had to rely on his instincts in a situation like this, and his instincts were telling him that Kafka posed no threat.

Kafka looked up and noticed the sun was beginning to descend. "Quick, we need to get to the Circle before the sun goes down. These groves can get a bit nasty in the dark."

With no more trepidation, Darien nodded his head

and picked up the pace. He did not know what lurked deeper in the green pastures, so he decided he best stick close to the creature. He could wait a while longer to get his answers. He knew now this was no dream. But little did he know, he was still in for a rude awakening.

Chapter 7
The Golden Circle

Darien and Kafka had been walking for some time. The island was pitch black, and if it hadn't been for the misty hue, they would not have even been able to see their immediate surroundings. In the dark, Darien's sense of smell was heightened. The scents of the plants, leaves and flowers had fused together into a smooth and intoxicating aroma. As soothing as the smell in the atmosphere was, the long walk from the shore was beginning to take its toll on Darien. His tux, still not dry, felt heavy on his body, and through sheer power of will he kept moving forward.

He could hear the sound of his breathing echo with every step. He grew anxious as his cold golden Rolex, a high school graduation gift from his mother, shot needles up his right wrist. He noticed it was stuck on 1:08—the time when Darien jumped into the water. He smiled at his frozen watch, reminded of his friend Kakoo's story about a bus ride he had shared with a Masai tribesman on the way to Kilimanjaro. Kakoo had noticed that the tribesman was wearing a watch that didn't work. When he brought it to the man's attention, his response was timeless. He said it wasn't working then, but one day it will work.

Could this all be a dream? Will my watch start working once I am awake? Darien thought to himself.

"Alright, we're almost there," an excited Kafka said.

Darien looked ahead and noticed a bright light like a bulb on a Christmas tree beyond the chaparrals before them. Darien was relieved. Civilization did exist on Ashkhas Island. When Kafka pushed the shrubs aside, what Darien saw next made him stop in his place and gasp.

Hundreds of kooky and supernatural creatures, of all shapes and sizes, stood scattered around a field. The bizarre assembly of the Ashkhasi dwellers was so diverse and equally so strange that it made Kafka look borderline normal. Darien's eyes widened as he took the complete spectacle in with pupils diluted.

"Whoa," Darien panted as he looked over the creatures.

"Welcome to the Golden Circle!" said Kafka.

This was his big opening line. All that were missing were a drumroll and an orchestra. But Darien stood as stiff as a stone, his jaw loose as his eyes roamed in shock. He could see everything clearly from his position just outside a halo made up of millions of gold particles hovering over the flat piece of land, which was the size of a football pitch.

As Kafka walked through the light, a glittering luminance seemed to rupture the halo, as it still stayed afloat. "Alright then, what are you waiting for? Come!" Kafka motioned for Darien to pass through the glimmering lit ring.

At this point, the abnormal was beginning to become normal for Darien. He proceeded through, spritzing gold dust all through the air. When he turned back, the floating Circle returned to its original shape again. Whether it was the radiance of the golden sprinkles or the warm bodies around, Darien was beginning to feel more at ease.

Scattered around the field, he noticed tiny fire places and little huts that looked like wooden pyramids with feet, hooves and paws of creatures shuffling around inside them. He saw normal animals amongst the Ashkhasi dwellers as well: chickens, ducks, and a few miniature-sized goats running around. He could not help but glance over at Kafka.

"Don't look at me. It's not like they're my kids!" Kafka shot back.

Darien smirked. "You really weren't kidding when you said Circle, this thing surrounding everyone is just floating a few feet over the ground."

"Well what would you have suggested we call it then?"

Darien smiled. He was beginning to warm up towards the furry man with a natural goatee. "You know Kafka, you're as quick with your tongue as you are with those clogs you call legs."

Kafka began to laugh hysterically. "Looks like you're finally coming around, Mr. Shams!"

Darien pointed to the creatures surrounding a large bonfire in the middle of the field. "What's going on there?"

Kafka said, "That my friend, is why we are here. Let's

go. Time for Evren to tell you everything you need to know." Kafka walked briskly towards an old man sitting at the fire, Darien just a few steps behind. "We're here, and just as you asked, mum was the word and I didn't say anything to him."

Darien looked at the man who must be Evren. Wrapped in a white garment, he looked freakishly human with a shaved head, wiry figure and a pleasant smile. He looked at Darien with a face void of any expression. Not a single wrinkle or twitch adorned on Evren's smile.

"You're finally here," Darien heard someone say. He thought it must have been one of the other fellers sitting around. The old man's lips had not moved. "I know what is going through your mind, young Darien."

Darien thought Evren must be in his head. With everything that was going around him, it surely was not too farfetched an idea.

"You must be trying to make sense out of it all," continued Evren, his smiling lips still sealed. "You are on Ashkhas Island. This much I can tell you is real. And everyone on this island is as real as you are."

Darien could not hold his curiosity in any longer. "How is it that I can hear you but I do not see your lips moving?"

"Well, that's because you are not looking at the right place," Evren said, lifting his hand off his knee to help himself get up. He stretched both his arms out from his sides.

Not knowing what to expect next, Darien felt jitters percolating down his spine. He nudged his left foot back a step and planted it firmly, ready to defend himself in case the old man decided to jump at him.

Evren opened the palm of his hands and said again, "because you are not looking at the right place."

And there it was, to Darien's astonishment, a pair of thin lips hollowed out inside his left palm. On his right was a single glistening grey eye. As Darien returned his gaze in awe to the old man's face, Evren lit up, his skin shining like the screens Darien had spent hours staring at in the office.

"Not everything is what it seems, Darien. Sometimes we reach a point where the only way out is the way forward."

Exasperated, Darien took a moment to sit down. It finally dawned on him, as he stared at the little sparkles jumping out of the fire and evaporating, that this could very well be happening. "This not a dream, is it?"

Evren sat opposite Darien. The light protruding from his skin went off as soon as he closed his fists. "No, it isn't a dream. And neither was the visit you had from Syoshant."

Darien coughed. "How do you know that? How did you know about my dream?"

Evren continued to smile. "It wasn't a dream. There is a lot I know about you."

Darien now was even more disoriented than when he had found himself washed ashore on the island.

"This is no accident. There are no such things as accidents. Only fate redesigned," Evren said, his hands resting on his knees. "You see us? There are a hundred and fourteen of us inside the Circle and we each serve a purpose. You, like us, are no different and bear a fate that needs to be fulfilled."

"What do you mean? What fate?" Darien asked.

"The premonition you had when you were a child was issued by the same voice that beckons you now to look at the greater good in the world every single day of your life." Evren paused to look around. In a quieter voice, he said, "We are cherubs of the virtuous and you, young Darien, are the world's guardian angel, assigned to protect all that is righteous and irreprehensible. You see, the world as we know it relies upon a balance between good and evil, all that stands for what is moral and immoral. We exist so as to preserve what we all collectively have defined as just."

Evren gave Darien a moment to grasp what he was saying and carried on.

"Not long ago, man grew a sense of conscience. He defined himself by what he is, what he thinks, and, more importantly, what he feels—failing to realize that all come from One single source. All of man's qualities come from One divine being. And that One being has bestowed nature's hand with the ability to balance itself. Where there is good, there is also evil. And where evil arises, so does good. But a deity on this very island has grown strong and aims to conquer the world with evil. And you, Darien Shams, just as others have before you, will need to stop that from happening for the sanctity of all that you know to be divine in this universe."

The other creatures sat quietly around the fire waiting

for Darien to say something, but Darien's mind had gone blank. The silence was deafening. Finally, he managed to ask, "Why me?"

Evren paused and the eyes of the others lit up in anticipation of what prudent choice of words the old wise man would make.

"Because Darien," Evren paused motionlessly and said. "You are awake. You are the son of the moment."

Evren then glanced over at Kafka and nodded, a cue that the conversation was done.

"Right!" Kafka said ecstatically. "First things first: we need to get you some fresh clothes and something to eat."

Too consumed by his own thoughts, Darien failed to hear Kafka. Taking deep breaths, he noted the night sky above the shimmering halo and the Ashkhasi inhabitants all adorned in white and black. He felt as if a stream of water were running through his arteries and cooling the blood vessels around his heart and spine. As shook up and bewildered as he was, he felt more exhilarated and alive in this moment of silence than he ever had before.

Darien felt he could sit there in silence for eternity. Thanks to Kafka though he would never know whether he had the Buddhist mettle to meditate in eternal serenity.

"Darien! Come on! On your feet, let's feed you!" said Kafka.

Darien looked at Evren, before climbing to his feet. "All those years growing up, I thought there was something wrong with me. And over the past few months, I was in a rut. I had given up on life, but, thanks to you, I now know I was not alone." Darien turned to Kafka and started to pat his clothes down from the dust that settled on them while sitting down. "Right Kafka, what are we having?"

ل

Chapter 8
Hubal

Storming through the other side of the woodland was Kayret.

He was a creature with no soul, the last of his kind on Ashkhas Island. He had no one to call family or friend because he was as treacherous as a Venus flytrap and had deceived his whole tribe out of sheer greed. Seeing his clan, known as the Datom growing in numbers had served as a threat to the perfidious Kayret.

His colony only fed on Dhubs, spiny-tailed lizards scattered all throughout the island. They grew large, some as big as a medium-sized dog, and had a menacing look like miniature dragons, but Dhubs were not the sharpest of creatures, not having evolved to naturally fend off predators. They were placid by nature and could only swing their long tail to hurt little creatures. Packed with blubber and meat, they made the perfect meal for the Datom clan, who stood mostly on their long hind legs but built up incredible speed on all four. They could chase a Dhub from almost a mile away. Their piercing eyes were filled with watery yellow pupils, which gave them extraordinary vision in both day and night time. Their ears, as long as a branch of a sapling palm tree were designed to make them perfect spies and scouts on Ashkhas. The Datom were the only creatures on the island who preyed on Dhubs, but as their numbers grew, the population of Dhubs dwindled. The elders, who included Kayret's father in their ranks, made a pact to ration what remained of the Dhubs on the island. Kayret though had other plans.

Through debauchery and deceit, he managed to convince the evil liege, Hubal that the Datom were conspiring against him by giving information about him to Evren and the Golden Circle's inhabitants. In retaliation, Hubal exterminated Kayret's entire clan, sparing only Kayret himself. He kept him only for the sole purpose of eavesdropping and spying on all who lived on the island.

Now Kayret had the most vital information at his disposal, something that the island had not witnessed in a very long time. He needed to deliver it to the right hand. And that was the golden hand of Hubal.

He ran as fast as he could, dashing through the jungle, breaking figs and slipping pass tree trunks with his slim frame and long limbs. He camouflaged into the red, orange and green leaves as he zoomed past them faster than the speed of sound. The trail became darker and more sinister with every marching gallop he took towards where Hubal stayed.

Kayret reached his destination, skidding across the entrance of the temple known as the Tomb. The massive stone building, where Hubal lived, stood in the middle of the jungle. It was manned by two armed soldiers from

Hubal's stout and indestructible army, a horde of three hundred and sixty soldiers known as the Yanissaries. It was the greatest battalion the world had ever seen. They had been locked up by Hubal for as long as time existed so as to be trained to demolish, kill and destroy anyone or anything instructed by Hubal himself. Even for Kayret who had been there countless times, the Tomb gave him shivers whenever he saw it. The two standing guard in front of the Tomb's wooden hatch instantly recognized the pesky Kayret and let the galling messenger pass inside. Kayret's veins were coursing with fear. He had no idea how the one who cast an eclipse on the sun would receive the news. He made his way to the second floor and gently knocked on the door, but his second knock loosened the door open.

Inside the murky room, Hubal stood next to a wide table with a hundred and fourteen candles on it that Hubal religiously kept lit. Each candle represented an Ashkhasi he was going to execute when the time came to fulfill his own fate.

"Kayret," he hummed quietly, his voice echoing as though he were standing at the bottom of a well.

"Yes, your highness," a quivering Kayret croaked.

"You know better than to show up uninvited to my domain," Hubal hissed with a voice deeper than a bottled thunderbolt.

Kayret was dead scared. He couldn't flinch. He started to gurgle and hesitatingly said, "Yes-yes, your supreme being, but-but…"

"But what? And to think you have had the nerve to

show up even when I have guests."

Kayret had been so engrossed by his fear that he had failed to see Cazi the witch and her son Fulad Zereh also in the room.

"Yes, yes, your holiness, but…"

Before Kayret could finish his sentence, Hubal pounced on him and squeezed him by the throat. "Silence! You speak only when I tell you to speak."

Hubal's face was now only inches away from Kayret. His elusive eyes were as white and as bright as the moon. His gnarled mouth displayed golden teeth against pale yellow skin. He squeezed Kayret's neck a little tighter and the long limbed Datom grasped Hubal's golden right hand, the hand that made him fearless and endowed him with invincibility.

Kayret was sure his time to join the rest of the Datom clan had arrived. Fighting for life, he tried to utter his last words in hopes of one more chance of survival. "The messiah has arrived!"

Hubal eased his grip. "What did you say, you little turd?"

Kayret repeated what he had said, still holding on dear life.

"Ha!" Hubal tossed Kayret to the side like a ragged cloth and looked over at Cazi. "Their savior has ascended. Tell me, Kayret, how did you hear of this savior's arrival?"

Kayret was rubbing his neck, trying to catch his breath on the floor, when suddenly he discharged his entire body's skin like a shedding reptile. A repulsive habit the Datom had when under severe stress.

Hubal started to laugh. "You get rid of your filth, or I will cut you from life's umbilical cord this very instant."

Frightened, the only thing Kayret could think to do was roll his dead skin and swallow it whole.

"Well improvised, little rodent. Now tell me, how did you hear of this savior?"

Cazi interjected to Hubal, "why do you keep him around?"

"Because any being that is diabolic enough to murder his own family is good in my book," Hubal replied with a devilish smile whilst looking at Cazi and pointing at Kayret with his glistening golden hand. "Now, go on you little pest, or I will have my fingers choke the life out of you."

"Well-well, I was inspecting the island for you master, I was looking for anything that could come of use for you." Kayret said as his knees buckled failing to stand up straight to respect Hubal's menacing presence.

"Ha ha ha, don't test me by lying!" said Hubal as he looked over his candles. "Just say you were scavenging the jungle in search of those diminutive Dhubs you are so obsessed with, you little pest."

"Well, yes. Yes, your majesty. I promise. I promise I won't lie again." Kayret was so nervous he would probably end up repeating every other word. He then carried on telling Hubal how he had seen Darien with Kafka, and watched him long enough to see him enter the Golden Circle and sit with Evren.

Cazi and Fulad Zereh got enraged when they heard Evren's name. Cazi was endowed with spellbinding powers. However the witch was cursed in one matter: she had failed to defeat her oldest adversary, Evren. Their history had only grown viler over the course of the many years since. Both Cazi and her son Fulad Zereh had been seeking vengeance on Evren for centuries. And Fulad, Cazi's only son, could by sheer strength alone stand against Hubal's indestructible three hundred and sixty strong, but lacked even one iota of brain power. All brawn and no brain made Fulad both an asset and a risk to Hubal's long-awaited kismet.

Hubal, on the other hand, was only growing stronger, the gold on his hand shining brighter as the years, decades and centuries passed. He had his own prophecy to fulfill. He was to set the world ablaze and take his army and henchmen across the island on a trail of carnage, misery and pain. His only motivation was to tilt the balance in favor of the evil that brewed inside his soul. His very existence hinged on bringing about this one revelation for the billions who roamed planet earth.

"So Darien, the anointed one, has arrived?" said Hubal, intrigued by the name and curious about what the one sent to defeat him might look like.

"I'll make sure to look right into his soul when he tastes the serrated edge of my sword."

"Are we not going to do anything about it?" Cazi asked Hubal in surprise.

"Do anything? Don't you know, Cazi? The messiah arrives when it is already too late. He arrives when doomsday has already struck." He then looked at each one of them. "We stick to my ordained plan. Fulad, you know what you need to do."

Fulad let out a blaring howl and stormed out of the room.

Chapter 9
Abtu & Anet

Fulad Zereh's scurrying had sent a tremble across the entire island. He was an imposing figure and, when he ran, his stomps would inflict pain on the ground he strode upon. His lack of stealth had set off an alarm for two particular fish by the names of Abtu and Anet.

"Anet, did you pick that up?"

"I did," Anet replied, just as terrified as Abtu was.

The two were almost identical, each garnished with fish scales that shined like emeralds in prismatic colors. Their fusiform bodies, with long flukes stretching behind them as far as their entire bodies, were designed for superior swimming. Their flukes, in fact, were the only way to distinguish between them: Anet's fluke had symmetrical lesions coiling upwards, Abtu's on the other hand spiraled downwards. Evren was the only one who could easily spot this difference. He was also the one who taught them how to speak *Lisan*, the language which Darien had magically acquired when arrived. Lisan was a tongue native only to the Ashkhasi, but any land dwelling being that laid foot on the island would be able to speak it. What was special about Abtu and Anet was that they were the only water-born animals that understood the Lisan tongue.

When they were baby fry, Evren came across them one day as he was walking along the shoreline. Abtu had been washed ashore wrapped in a weave of algae and sea grass and flapping frantically. From the water Anet was trying to bite down on his companion's fluke in order to drag him back into the water.

Evren stood and watched. As much as it bothered him, he knew he should let nature take its course. But just as he was ready to move past them, he heard Anet yell out Abtu's name and knew instantly that they were no ordinary fish. He also knew he was no random pedestrian and that this was an omen he could not ignore. He freed Abtu and then showed up every morning thereafter to teach them Lisan. Years later when they both had learnt how to speak, Anet asked Evren why he chose to help them that day.

Evren's response was "The real miracle was not that you spoke, but that you risked your own life to save your brother's."

And from that day on, the two brothers swore to keep Evren and the inhabitants of the Golden Circle safe from the evil dwellers of the island.

"We need to make a move," said Abtu now, knowing they had to get to Evren and warn the rest of the Ashkhasis' allies as soon as they could. From the day Abtu and Anet were saved, they became two of the Ashkhasis' few emissaries. The preservation of the island's conduct of life lied with each inhabitant. And so it was by an unspoken bond that every creature on land or water in

Ashkhas worked together to defend the island's moral sanctity.

"Let's hurry then. We'll have to swim around the island," Anet replied. "By the time we get there it might be too late!"

They were endowed with another gift as well. They had the ability to pick up sonar frequencies hundreds of miles away. They had very tiny ear openings but behind those slits were a cavity that was as strong as a satellite. They could echolocate the exact pinpoint location of any object as long as they picked up the frequencies. And these dense oscillating sonar beams were the marching stomps of one Fulad Zereh which gave the two brothers all that they needed to know.

The fish dashed like two radiating precious stones on a sling shot leaping frequently into the air to reduce time spent fighting the friction of the water. They needed to get to the Golden Circle. They needed to get to Evren.

Chapter 10
The Attack

On the other side of the island, Darien had built up quite the appetite walking from the shore to the Circle. He found a perfectly situated rock to sit on just by the Circle, giving him the chance to ravage four plates of Dolmas— grape leaves wrapped around a stuffing blend of meat, dill and rice—and swing his hands through the perimeter to watch the gold-coated dust scatter all over him. And even though it struck his curiosity to do so, he was too busy entertaining himself like a kid with a foaming bubble toy to bother asking what the golden dust actually was.

A few empty plates lay right next to him. The Dolmas also had other herbs that his palettes were unable to figure out. Whatever else was in them, he did not seem bothered as he found them delectable. "These little things are good, Kafka," he said while waving his hand once again through the gilt that was the Golden Circle.

"I wish I could say the same," Kafka replied. "But I don't think Evren's idea of noble traits includes cannibalism, so I would not know how they taste."

Darien's face dropped immediately.

"Relax! Relax!" Kafka chanted. "You're so stunned your face just started to run towards your forehead!"

The world Darien came from cannibalism was no laughing matter. Was this an Ashkhasi on his plate? Is that what Kafka meant? Darien felt like spitting the last chunk of Dolma he had in his mouth out.

"It's a joke, Darien," Kafka continued. "You have got to keep up with my jokes, oh dear furless savior. That's just goat meat you're having. I think it would be weird if I were to eat it myself considering the uncanny resemblance I may have to them."

"Furless savior, huh? That's funny," Darien replied.

At least now he knew that the meat in Dolmas on Ashkhas Island was mutton. There was a childlike quality to Kafka's behavior that Darien was beginning to enjoy. It reminded him of how he would joke around with Samer when they would sit at bars or cafes and crack jokes until late at night while chain smoking their lungs out. It also reminded him that he had not lit up a cigarette or even had the urge to light one since he arrived on the island. It was a blessing. He could smell and taste once again. He was able to pick up on the harmony brewing in the air, a freshness his lungs had not savored in a very long time. The cool scents flowing from the water and the musk radiating from all of the different herbs and plants awakened emotions Darien had hidden deep inside. The sweet savory aroma took him back to the age of five, when he would ask his mother to make him rolled-up butter and cheese sandwiches on a piece *Lavash*, a soft thin flatbread popular amongst Iranians, Turks, Armenians and the Caucasus. He had always asked his mother to spread the butter first, and when she was in a hurry and forgot to do so, he would somehow know even if she tried to hide it by flipping the sandwich. They had always reminisced of his butter-then-cheese infatuation and laughed about it.

His mother—she must be worried, he thought to himself. Everyone at the wedding. What a dent he must have put in his best friend's big day. The last thing he ever wished for was to put anyone through any misery. But fate had placed him here at this very moment and his will was reinforced by the knowledge that he had a destiny to fulfill. The messianic thoughts he had had as a kid all of sudden didn't seem childish. This was the real deal. Darien looked up and noticed the sun beginning to dawn. The night had not lasted long, or so it had felt. And just as the sun crested the horizon, he asked God to give him the courage to go through with this.

While deep in thought, he heard Kafka joking around with Tanit, who Darien had got to know earlier. She was as elegant and pristine as a lotus flower. Even though her skin was pale and bright like the moon at night, she was still a very attractive Ashkhasi. Tanit offered to take his Dolma plates away. This was something that Darien was beginning to notice. Everybody contributed. Unlike in the world he came from, these island inhabitants seemed to understand that a hundred and fourteen pairs of hands are much more effective than one.

He kept silent for a moment longer, looking at Kafka scratch figs off of his hooves. He needed to ask him a question. "Tell me something," he said. "How does…" he paused. "How does…ah never mind."

"Never mind?" replied Kafka, who was now curious. "Never mind and you cease to exist. You are what your mind creates. So go on, I can handle any question you swing my way. I've got thick skin, well, at least from the navel below," he joked.

"Ok, here it goes." Darien took a deep breath and leaned forward towards Kafka. "How do relationships work with you guys?" he figured if he threw in a bit of subtlety it would make his lascivious question more appropriate.

"What do you mean? We exist because we each serve a purpose. Weren't you listening to what Evren said?" Kafka replied.

"What I mean is…" Darien paused again. "Well from where I'm standing, it looked like you were flirting with Tanit, so how does that work?"

"For someone who has been ordained with the divine destiny to establish the new covenant between all of humanity and God, you have a hard time expressing yourself!" said Kafka. He shrugged his shoulders. "I mean your words are harder to crack than the trunk of a palm tree. Just get to the point already!"

"Damn it, do I have to spell it out?" Darien was agitated that Kafka thought he might not have heard what Evren had said earlier about the destiny he had to fulfill. "Let me put it this way then, how do you procreate? How do you decide who you mate with? If you like someone, or fall in love, how do you decide to be with them?" Darien went on shooting a barrage of questions. "Is that clear enough for you now?"

Kafka's eyes swelled up. "Procreate? Procreate? Darien, does it look like I procreate? I don't wear pants!" he continued, pointing at his flossy and woolly legs. "See, that's the problem with your kind. Everything for you stems from a physical need. Most of you think with either your belly or what's below it." Kafka looked stunned, as Darien, who the very salvation of mankind hinged on, could only think of asking about procreation. "I am not one to judge. But it seems like for the inhabitants of earth outside this island, all of your actions stem from a primal urge that you can only think to fulfill through physical, emotional or mental stimuli."

Darien was a little dumbfounded with what Kafka was saying.

"We don't operate that way. We, the Ashkhasis, have no free will. We cannot act on our urges. Now let me ask you a question. Do you know how many people roam this earth today?"

"Yeah, more than seven billion," Darien said, quick to reply to Kafka's pop quiz.

"Ok, do you know how many people have roamed the earth to date?"

Darien could not think of an answer. "I don't know, enlighten me."

"Over one hundred and seven billion," Kafka replied. "You keep regenerating because you have the urge to improve. That is the makeup of your DNA. But we do not. We are evolved. We do not need to conquer. We do not need to waste. We do not kill by choice. And we certainly do not need to fornicate when we misinterpret the concept of love." He paused. "I love the sand your feet are resting on just as much as I love Tanit. I love Evren just as much as I love those little fish you see swimming through that stream of water."

Darien followed the direction of Kafka's pointing hands to a stream of fresh water running right through the field.

"So you see, love for us who dwell on Ashkhas is life and every living form in it. Love liberates us from all primal urges and it is because of our lack of free will and complete submissiveness that we understand it in its purest form. What you call flirting is nothing more than a way to show our love."

Darien wanted to share his own interpretation of love. He had thought he was in love with Mariam until a rude awakening made him realize that love would not set him free. It would only shackle him. But before he could carry the conversation further, Kharteet, a gigantic Ashkhasi with fists the size of wrecking balls interrupted them.

"Darien, Evren sent me to give you a fresh set of clothes," said Kharteet with his protruding belly about a foot away from Darien's face. The bulge was so large that, losing its battle with gravity, it almost dangled to the ground.

Darien was so used to wearing wet clothes from the gym that he had also forgotten he was still in his tux. His white shirt which had begun to shrivel with dried salt water looked like it was iron pressed by then.

Not giving Darien a chance to respond, Kafka was quick to say, "Kharteet, you startled us. If only you were as good at hiding your appetite as you are yourself!"

Darien had noticed how the two maintained strict eye contact when addressing one another. It was very common in his world, when people wanted to take jabs at each other but were either too ashamed or had some hidden agenda, to look at one another in the eye for long. Here, though, it showed how lighthearted everybody was.

"Very funny," Kharteet replied. He could not help but laugh along with Kafka.

Before he knew it, Darien was laughing along with them. "Sure Kharteet, what do you need from my side?"

"Simple really, just stand up and put your arms out."

Darien got up and Kharteet started to measure his wingspan, hips, chest and legs. It turned out to be an awkward exercise, Kharteet's body only allowing him to get so close to Darien without bumping into him. Darien then turned to Kafka, thinking he could squeeze one more cheeky comment in. "Guess you're not that evolved then. Still need to stitch your clothing, huh?"

Before Kafka had a chance to respond, Kharteet drummed his belly, clapped his hands like a pair of church bells and spun Darien around by the ends of his shirt, picking up dust and branches. Figs started flying around. And before he could look down, Darien was dressed in a set of fresh threads. He was now fitted in the same black outfit that everybody else wore—well, except Kafka and Evren. The soft-soled leather boots that almost reached to his knees were comfortable, and the sleeves of his coat were loose but tight around his wrists. The waist was taped with a tight belt holding a skirt onto the pants that went under the boots. The skirt was unconventionally comfortable like the kilts he wore a few times during the year he lived in Edinburgh. The chest came equipped with holsters that were fitted with tiny glass tubes filled with the same gold dust hovering around the field.

Darien took out one of the vials with the golden dust out its holster on his chest and shook it incessantly. He found their color alluring. He thought of how Kafka just a moment ago gave this profound speech on the Ashkhasis' idea of love and its universality, yet even they differentiated between male and female. His whole attire, and that of the men in the Circle, was completely black, while the women were dressed in elegant white dresses and knitted jackets. The jackets were fastened with a golden silhouette and the skirts had a slit at the front to give them more mobility. The women's attire also came accessorized with varying golden and silver beads, coins, delicate pendants or necklaces. And in the span of the past few hours, Darien had seen all sorts of embroideries.

"Alright then, Darien, give it a go!" Kharteet said, stepping backwards to give Darien some space.

Darien dashed in short spurs from side to side, realizing how agile the clothes made him feel even on a full stomach.

"You wear it very well, Darien," said Evren as he walked towards them.

"Thank you. I have to admit, it feels pretty comfortable." Darien smiled at Evren's compliment.

Evren thanked Kafka and Kharteet for their help, and asked Darien to join him for a stroll. Darien promptly obliged and moved by his side as they began to walk across the field. He could feel the wind's hiss brush against his new clothes as they walked. He grabbed his long locks and wrapped them in a bundle behind his head's crown.

Evren looked up and pointed at the sun to Darien. "Darkness is nothing more than the destitute of light. I am sure you noticed how our nights are much shorter than our daylights." Evren paused and Darien could hear Evren's breath under his words.

"One cannot exist without the other."

Darien could not come up with anything to say. Evren's steps seemed to mute all the other noises around them. The shuffling of feet, the ear-pecking clucks from the chicken and the sporadic words echoing all around them got more silent with each step.

"The instant you were born and took your first breath, you were summoned to be a part of this holy crusade," Evren continued.

"An evil brute grows strong and now is on the verge of crossing over from the island to the world you know. His name is Hubal, and his strength grows as your world's lightness folds." Evren's voice was wrapped in despair. It seemed as though he bore the world's pain on his shoulders, even though his smile and gentle eyes gave the impression he was content with all he had seen and experienced. "Your world is in a state of dystopia. Dishonesty has become the acceptable way of life. Men and women have sold their faith for worldly gains. Respect for each other no longer exists. People have fallen back on idol worshipping and money is the new shrine. Vice and immorality are celebrated. People are killed and robbed of the chance to live on earth by the hands of those whose core is built from evil. Righteousness is holding on a thin thread today." Evren stopped walking and turned to face Darien. "That is why you have felt so disconnected all this time. It wasn't your work. It wasn't your pursuit of companionship. It wasn't your life but rather what was transpiring around you. Those thoughts you had as a child were no accident. You are the soul through which life pulsates. When the world is miserable, so are you. When the world rejoices, so do you. You have been requested to usher in the new rule of God and usher out the old rule of man. This is your holy crusade."

Darien's mind started to race. "But why me? Those thoughts and dreams I had were nothing more than the works of a child's imagination, Evren. Why have I been chosen?"

"Because Darien, you have borne the world's discontent since childhood. These circumstances were thrust upon you so as to make you feel completely empty, and so you stopped seeing all that is beautiful in the world. It is only when your heart is completely drained that you will grow the desire to fill it. But you occupied yourself with such insignificant matters as you got older that you lost sight of it. Now the time has come for you to submit yourself to the good you have felt throughout the years. And you yourself know that. When your father, your own flesh and blood, cusses you and exiles you from his soul's house. When the woman you selected decides to seek comfort from other men. When your colleagues lie and cheat for material gains. When your world's men and women of power kill others for their belief, you know something is not right."

Darien could no longer see or hear any of his surroundings. Evren's words were pouring through him as though they were his own.

"This is the moment where truth crosses with your destiny and you have the chance to right these wrongs."

Darien could feel the energy gush through his veins. He felt as though his pores were exuding light under his new clothes. He clinched his fists as a tide of vitality convulsed down his spine and through his entire body.

He was the five-year-old boy again.

"What do I need to do, Evren?"

"People hold an immense power. And that is the power of choice. We do not, so there are certain things we cannot do. But you can."

"And what certain thing do I need to do?" he asked, wanting to quickly unlock the safe to fulfillment.

"We by nature cannot kill. And that is the only way Hubal can be stopped." Evren deliberately paused to see what Darien might say. Hearing nothing, he continued. "The earth's disarray has given Hubal the strength to conquer its inhabitants, and he plans to do so. None of us is a match for him. Even if one was, he could not take Hubal's life. But the sons and daughters of Adam can. You have forces that want to see you defeat him. And to defeat him you will have to call upon Alicanto, a divine bird that is the only creature that can break Hubal's invincibility."

"You need to get to Tavara Hill. There you will find the Zomorod Box. In it is the Ayna, a powerful mirror in which, when the sun reflects upon it, Alicanto appears. Once Alicanto arrives and makes Hubal vulnerable, that is when your window of opportunity opens to…"

"…take Hubal's life away." said Darien, finishing Evren's sentence off.

"We can help you get to Tavara Hill. Everything else that unravels from that point on is in your hands," said Evren.

Darien was having trouble coming to terms with the extremity of what Evren was saying. The world's continued existence hinged on him taking another being's life. He wanted to reach out and ask a more esoteric question: was taking a life righteous itself? But he knew this was not the time nor the place.

"And there is one more thing. This is for you," said Evren as he took out something wrapped around a piece of fur, which he unrolled. The decorative plate within shone light right into Darien's eyes. Fused with an array of colors and bursting with gold dust, it was an oblong shield with a crest bearing a square with four gates, each containing a circle.

"What is that?" enquired Darien.

"This right here is the Mandala shield."

Evren no longer needed to emphasize what the journey ahead entailed; Darien was beginning to get the drift. This wasn't a Sudoku puzzle. Things were going to get dangerous, and there would be definitive life or death consequences.

"Hold on to this for it will keep you safe. It is made up of Rumla, the same matter you see all around us," said Evren. He handed the shield to Darien.

"What if I fail? What will happen then?" said Darien as he looked down into his own reflection on the shield.

"That, young Shams, nobody knows. You do what has been asked and let the One above take care of everything else."

They then noticed a horde of the Ashkhasis gathering around the nearby stream.

"Something is not right," said Evren. He ran towards the crowd with Darien trailing him.

Tussling and jumping out of the water were Abtu and Anet.

"We heard Fulad storming towards here!" Abtu yelled.

"Quick everyone!" Evren yelled with a garish, strong voice. Even though he appeared an old man, Evren had an uncanny resilience with reflexes to match. "Let's remain vigilant and ready. Our Lord will forgive us for what our spears will not!"

"Darien!" said Kafka as he ran towards Darien and tugged on his sleeve. "Stay close, stay right next to me. Things go get rough."

The Ashkhasis started to run around and the ground began to rhythmically tremble. It got stronger with every passing moment. Little stones and leaves were bouncing off the earth with every pulse. Darien's heart started to race.

Before anybody could react, a behemoth of a creature shattered through the Golden Circle. It was Fulad Zereh. And Darien was in complete awe of what he saw. The creature's plod was so powerful that a few including Darien fell to the ground. From his side, he took a good look at Fulad. The creature seemed to be made completely of what appeared to be metal to Darien's eyes. His massive legs looked sturdier than the trunk of a thousand-year-old tree, and though they were as large as elephants, he was as nimble and agile as a gazelle.

Koshti, a strong, simian looking Ashkhasi regarded as their strongest warrior, was the first to lead the defensive attack as he leapt onto Fulad's back. But the endeavor proved futile. Fulad just tossed him aside like a strand of hair with his shimmering steel-plated arm. Throughout the melee, Darien had tripped and fallen on his back. He quickly got back to his feet and gripped his shield tight, his eyes locking with Fulad. Fulad knew all of the Ashkhasis and seemed to instantly recognize him.

"You don't have much time, Kafka!" yelled out Evren. "Take Darien away from here! Take him to Tavara Hill!"

Darien did not budge. He had grown up with the sound of bombs from the Iran and Iraq war, and his instincts in this moment were telling him to stand and fight. As he planted his feet firm on the soft sand, Fulad started to charge towards him. Darien locked his jaw and held his shield in front of his chest, but Evren had other plans. The old man jumped right in front of Fulad, somehow stopping the creature cold.

"Darien! Go! Run! Remember what I told you!" yelled Evren.

Darien had no time to think clearly. All hell had broken loose, Fulad's glimmering coat now eclipsed by the numerous Ashkhasi bodies upon him. He was so caught up in the moment that the only thing Darien could feel was Kafka pulling him back into the wilderness.

ن

Chapter 11
The Sword of Zulfiqar

Darien and Kafka tore through the jungle, running until none of the tremors and screams could be heard.

"What was that thing?" Darien asked, slowing to a halt.

Kafka endeavored to tell the story of Evren and Fulad Zereh. The two had a long history. Before Hubal's kingdom of darkness, Cazi was the undisputed ruler. Her demise from the throne of power came at the hands of Evren. Her magic spells were not powerful enough and she had failed where Hubal was looking to succeed and that was to conquer the lands known to man. She was a gifted sorceress, but a lousy leader and tactician. Instead of planning to cross the island and enforcing the rule of evil on man, she first wanted to kill the Ashkhasis that dwelled in the Golden Circle. This ultimately ended up being her demise as Evren forcefully defended the Circle's inhabitants. She was consumed with vengeance and the desire to kill Evren for dethroning her ever since. The years passed and her taste for retaliation only grew. It was not long until she gave birth to a son, Fulad Zereh, on whom she cast a spell, endowing him with an impenetrable skin making him almost as invincible as Hubal. Cazi built a black well and showered Fulad in it. After he was raised out of it, he was engulfed in skin made of matter sturdier than steel. He was indestructible. His taste for blood was even stronger than his mother's. Her spite of Evren grew in him, and he promised her that he would avenge her loss someday. Today had been Fulad's chance to fulfill that promise, with blood in his eyes.

"We have to go back," Darien said.

"Go back? Did you see how big that walking Samovar was?" replied Kafka.

"I don't care, we can't just leave!" Darien said. He was beginning to believe Syoshant's prophecy, and no longer wanted to run away from his battles. But Kafka did not even seem worried that a beast like Fulad had just attacked his comrades.

"Evren told you," said Kafka, as though he needed to remind Darien of the bigger picture. "You need to get the Zomorod Box."

"That can wait, we need to go help the rest," replied Darien.

"Look Darien, Fulad has an impenetrable skin. There is nothing except…"

"Except what?" Darien was becoming impatient.

"Except one specific sword. A sword that can even tear the sun in half," said Kafka.

"Where is this sword?" said Darien.

"The sword of Zulfiqar is a perfect fusion of power and function, made of copper and bronze with an earthy material known as Virdama. It was molted and then cooled off in a mystic fountain by an Ashkhasi named Aruha. The legend goes that Aruha recited the name of God in every known language to man a million times while forging and hammering away on its henna-colored blade. The sword has a soul in its own. It bears the four elements that constitute life: earth, air, fire and water. It is in the graveyard of Tur, and hasn't been touched for as long as I can remember," replied Kafka, a bit spooked. The mere thought of either the sword or the graveyard seemed to give him the chills. Darien, on the other hand, was confused.

"Graveyard? I thought the inhabitants of Ashkhas don't die?"

Darien's question seemed to make Kafka feel even more uncomfortable. "The graveyard's not for us. It's for those who came before you."

"What do you mean before me?"

"I mean this isn't the first time a human has been called to stop the ruler of the dark kingdom. We Ashkhasis don't die, but we do pass away. Your concept of death and life is just as misconstrued as procreation. Every living being that breaths will for certain pass away at one point in time."

Darien was growing weary of Kafka judging man. Every time he asked something it was met with rhetoric. This moment called for action.

"I'll tell you what I do know. If we don't get that sword and head back to the Circle, your peers or friends or whatever you call them will die. Do you want that?"

117

Darien stuck his chest out. "Tell me where I need to go to get this sword!"

"I wouldn't be worried about the rest if I were you though," replied Kafka.

"What do you mean? Did you see how he threw Koshti off his back? I think the rest could use all the help they can get," Darien replied.

"Well, you saw the Rumla floating around the field, right? It just doesn't glide around for your amusement! The Rumla helps us shift." Kafka paused. "Or as you call it, teleport. It teleports us to another area on the island. And the beautiful part is it only shifts us and nobody else. That's why Evren was more concerned about getting you away from the melee more than everybody else."

It dawned on Darien now that Kafka had such a level headed attitude because he knew the rest would be safe from harm. He was instantly relieved to know that the Rumla, the gold dusts hovering over the field served a larger purpose than for his sheer playful nature.

"I'm not too worried, all it takes is for eight Ashkhasis to jump simultaneously and yell out *Ourouboros!*" said Kafka as he leapt up in the air on both legs.

"Ourouboros?" replied Darien with one eyebrow up.

"I don't even know what it means," replied Kafka, scratching his head. "But it works!"

"You know, you could've saved your breath with all of that jazz about life and death if you just said they were all safe from the beginning!" said Darien with a sneer.

"Jazz?" Kafka looked puzzled.

"Never mind. I think we should still go get the sword.

We won't know when we will cross paths with Fulad again."

Kafka was not too keen on going to the graveyard, but he bowed his head and pointed towards its direction. "Fine, let's make a move then."

As they begun to briskly walk, Darien asked, "So there were others before me?"

"Yes, there were."

"What happened to them?"

"Some fulfilled the prophecy. And others didn't."

Darien was even more mystified. Figuring out the Ashkhasis was like leveling up on Candy Crush. Things just kept getting trickier as they made progress. Why had nothing ever been recorded of this surreal island. Why was it that others had come before yet no one had ever heard of any of the rumblings on Ashkhas Island?

"So if others failed, how come your evil force never made it off the island?" said Darien.

"Oh they did alright. Who do you think Genghis Khan was? Or Hitler? Or Saddam? I can go on!" replied Kafka while counting those three on his right hand. "Hubal is different though. He is set on not only destroying your world, but conquering it. He wants to fill the void you all have left with your lack of belief in God."

Darien knew what Kafka was talking about. Everybody he knew who claimed to be educated, well-versed and intelligent had bought into the trend of disbelieving in God. It seemed to be the hip thing to do. People were punished when they still believed in God and a religious institution. His generation ridiculed those who believed in God, labeling them as backward, naïve and fanatical. If devout Muslims stood for their religion, they were coined terrorists. If a Christian stood for Christ, they were labeled self-righteous. And if Jews preached about their beliefs, they were called Zionists.

"We just can't get it right can we, Kafka?" said Darien.

"Now what do you mean?" replied Kafka.

"Well there was a time when people were punished for not believing in God. Now they are punished for believing in it."

"It's not my place to judge, but your history would definitely agree with you," said Kafka.

"So what about those who failed? What happened to them?"

"They died."

"You mean passed away," Darien smirked.

The two were building a rapport, a friendship. Each was just as quick to throw in sarcastic jabs and beginning to enjoy the other's presence. Kafka pointed out a plush array of bamboo shoots before a hill. Beyond it lay the graveyard of Tur. Next thing he knew, he saw Darien race towards it.

"Here we go," bellowed out Kafka as he started to run along Darien. "Stop Darien! You need to slow down. We are not alone here," murmured Kafka as quietly as he could. "The graveyard has a guardian beast."

But Kafka's words fell on deaf ears as Darien, immersed in the moment, burst through the shoots. He could hear his own heart beat in rhythm with his steps. He could hear birds squawking from a distant place, crickets singing the symphony of nocturnia and, loudest of all, a growl that seemed like the sound of a thousand lions roaring. His curiosity, as with every young man with a mission, got the best of him. He had to take a look to see where this loud reverberation came from.

"No, stop. Let's think for a second," said Kafka.

He reached for Darien, but the boy pulled his arm away from Kafka's grip. Stepping into the open plain he saw a myriad of tombstones scattered beside a small hillside slope. The tombstones were made out of simple limestone that measured up to Darien's height. They bore no names. No dates. No prayers. No Crescents. No Crosses. No Stars of David.

Almost instantly, the beast was charging towards Darien, grumbling so loud the leaves came crashing down from the nearby trees. This was Ghoul, the protector of whom Kafka was trying to alert Darien. He resembled a hyena, but was larger than an elephant. His fur stood rigid on his back, his paws were equipped with claws the size of Darien's head. With just a few strides he had reached Darien, opening his jaws so wide it cast a shadow over the young man. Darien's instincts took over. Spotting an opening under the beast's wide torso, Darien slid under Ghoul to avoid his bone-crushing bite. But Ghoul turned with one swift motion and cocked his enormous skull back. He was gathering enough bite force to cut Darien into pieces with fangs the size of a rhinoceros' horns.

Kafka came to his aid, grabbing a small rock and throwing it at Ghoul's head to distract him. The monster now turned his attention to Kafka. Darien realized that he had no chance to overpower Ghoul physically. The old mantra of brains over brawls was what needed to be applied. But he needed to buy time.

"Kafka! Run to the other side, you need to distract him!" yelled Darien.

Ghoul began stomping towards Kafka, whose frightened hooves began to beat on the floor like he was a tap dancer. Running towards a tree that stood taller than the rest, he gathered all his energy and started to climb its elongated trunk. Darien knew he needed to act quickly. He looked around at the many rows of gravestones. He could use them as a maze to get the overgrown canine dizzy and throw him off balance. But he needed the sword.

Then he saw it next to one of the tombstones with a large eye plastered right in the middle. The sword of Zulfiqar was bound by two hooks right under the eye on the tombstone, and decorated with bright blue and green stones on its handle.

Ghoul was shredding the tree trunk Kafka was in like it was made out of papier-mâché. Without a moment to spare, Darien switched the shield over to his left hand and grabbed the sword with the other. He started screaming like a madman to grab Ghoul's attention and braced himself to run through the planted tombstones. Ghoul caught up with him with just a few wide strides, but was a clumsy beast and lost his footing. He smashed right into Darien and in a flash Darien was airborne, his fall broken on a bed of dead leaves and twigs. His chest was bursting with pain. Darien felt like a pipe had been dragged right through it. As he battled for air, he saw Ghoul towering over him ready to send Darien to the same place where others who failed before him had gone.

That split second felt like eternity, until his hand suddenly felt the cold blade of the sword right next to him which flew into the air and landed right next to him. He looked right into Ghoul's eyes, gripped the sword and sliced the creature's neck. The sword cut Ghoul's throat like a knife through melting butter. Ghoul started to stumble backwards. As ghastly a creature as he was, he was gracious in his moment of death. His roars now transmuted to sounds like the cries of an ailing child.

"Oh God," Darien sobbed, realizing what he had done. He threw his shield and sword to the ground.

As the last breaths left his body, Ghoul looked gentle and harmless. Darien, breathing heavy from the furor that just took place, could not help but be dispirited for what he had just done. He stood next to the motionless beast until Kafka had climbed down from the tree and placed his hand on his shoulder.

"Come Darien, we need to go back to the Circle."

Chapter 12
The Loss of an Ashkhasi

There was no funeral ceremony for Ghoul.

"I have never taken a life, so I can only imagine how you must feel," said Kafka sympathetically as they made their way back.

"I know Kafka, it just threw me off how one moment you have this enraged predator and the next he is nothing more than timid prey."

Kafka nodded his head. After what had transpired, the normally outspoken creature remained quiet.

This wasn't the first time Darien had killed a living being. It was by far the largest, but as a child he had a sadistic habit of torturing animals. His victims ranged from stray cats to rodents to reptiles and most notably crustaceans. As a child growing up in Dubai, his family would take frequent weekend trips to Hatta, a beautiful mountain range in the north of the country which oozed with wildlife. He would take plastic bags with him on his family excursions and fill them up with frogs, tadpoles and sea snails. Once back home with his victims, he would turn his own bath tub into a prison aquarium. His favorite muse was tying the frogs to threads and spinning them in his bathroom like a helicopter. He would get a thrill seeing the frogs and their decapitated limbs fly around his bathroom. If it wasn't for his mother, only God knows how much longer he would have fed his barbaric thirst for his ensuing bloodbath. It was not until one of their trips back from Hatta when his mother noticed a pungent smell consume their car on their way to Dubai that put a halt to his torturous ways. Darien had failed to tie one of his death chambers properly and the plastic bag had burst open freeing all of his victims who cried out for help by releasing their natural odor. His mother was infuriated. She never thought her boy could display such a vicious and dark side. And from that incident on, he was banned from taking anything from Hatta or even owning a pet.

But the worst of all was a torture he enacted at the age of fourteen involving a stray cat at the forest their house lay in the outskirts of Moscow. He took the free spirited animal into the wild and placed it in a box. With him, he had a ten liter jerrycan filled with petrol, which he stole from his father's toolshed. He showered the cat in petrol and after a few seconds lit it up and watched it run amok and burn to the ground. It haunted him for a long time, but he liked to blame it on rage built during his captive years in Russia.

The demise of Ghoul was different. Darien knew he could not bear the heart of a killer. Or at least he thought so. He believed death was a rite only reserved for God and the person who bore the soul. Who was he to take a life? Ghoul was doing nothing else but defending his turf. Did the beast deserve to die for his cause? It gave him a glimpse into understanding the Ashkhasi inhabitants and the destiny he was ordained to fulfill. They could not mount the will to kill.

Would that be his role? Was he the Hand of the Universe that would slay Hubal when the rest could not? Darien knew that the decimation of his world could only be avoided by him confronting Hubal and preventing him from crossing the island. And Ghoul, well he was what the lamb was to Abraham.

Just a sacrifice.

"How will you find the rest if they shifted from the previous spot?"

"Easy," said Kafka as he reached into the satchel hanging around his chest and took out a rusty old coin and a little glass tube filled with Rumla. He paused to look at Darien and his new clothes. "Actually, why waste this!"

He grabbed the coin and started rubbing it on the surface of Darien's shield until the Rumla, like glitter off of a postcard, dispersed into the air. Darien took a closer look and noticed an emblem of a falcon on the coin that instantly reminded him of the one *Dirham* coins he used to get as a kid. The little magical coins had given him the joy of buying anything his six-year-old heart desired. Whenever he got his hands on a few, he would run to the grocery store and indulge in packs of chips, chocolates and a bevy of little treats, which to him had been what he thought heaven tasted like.

The coin started to light up. The falcon on it came to life. It jumped off of the coin and stormed skyward letting out an eerie chant. Before Darien knew it, a blazing pathway was lit right under their feet and the bird had evaporated into the air.

"See. Magic!" said Kafka as he waited for Darien to show he was impressed by Kafka's own sorcery.

"Any other day and I would say this was the craziest thing I have seen," replied Darien. He was beginning to like the texture of the sword's grip in his hand. He slid the sword in between his shield's handles and got ready to move. "Alright then, let's get moving fast."

With no time to waste, they streamed forward across the lit trail with the sun wide awake above them. As he jogged, Darien reminisced of a day he had spent camping in the desert with his uncle, Ibrahim. *Ebi*, as everybody called him, was formerly a standout volleyball player who could've made a career out of his love for the sport. He played for the Iranian national team and competed at an international level. Unlike football or basketball, however, volleyball was never a mainstream sport so he never got the opportunity to play for a club and make an earnest living out of his true passion. He instead followed the family tradition and settled for a career in banking. For twenty years he served as a branch manager. It had gradually taken the life out of him. His uncle had always made sure to share with Darien that his heart was unfulfilled. He did not want to see his oldest nephew make the same mistake he did. His favorite story was the one about the most notorious Chinese general and Buddha. Looking up now at a sky of surreal colors, he could hear his uncle's voice reciting the story he had shared with him that day in the calm dunes of Dubai.

"'Oh! Buddha, I have conquered lands from the furthest point of the east all the way to the west. Tell me, have I been the most successful general mankind has ever seen?' Buddha replied, 'No.' He then pointed to one of the general's followers behind and said, 'He is.' To the general's astonishment, he told Buddha that he was nothing more than his chef, to which Buddha replied, 'Yes, but if he were to become general, he would have been the greatest general the world had ever seen.'"

Ebi made sure he drilled that into Darien's head. He wanted Darien to find out what his destiny was and fulfill it. *If only Ebi could see me now*, Darien thought to himself. He took one more glance above his head. The sky and its effervescent colors were hypnotic.

"It's beautiful, isn't it?" Kafka interjected.

"It is," replied a composed and introverted Darien. To him God's art was second to none. Everything man did was just poor imitation. And Darien always loved admiring the greatest artist's work whenever and wherever it was on display.

"Worth fighting for, isn't it?" Kafka continued, breathing heavily between each word.

"Down to the last breath," replied Darien as he too tried to pace his breathing. Darien had not done this much running since his days playing soccer at university. He was neither fatigued nor sore. He felt as though he could run for hours on end.

It was not long before the path led them to the Golden Circle. It was in shambles. All their belongings, which had a cuneiform with the word *Nisba* engraved on them that enabled them to be teleported as well, were scattered across the field. The huts, arranged in the form of a spiraling DNA helix, were destroyed, leaving only large sticks and palm leaves all over the place. The fireplaces, in particular the large one in the middle of the field, were put out.

As they entered the Circle, Darien heard cries of despair and angst.

"Is everyone ok?" a worried Kafka asked the first group he laid eyes on.

"Yes," replied a woman named Daena.

Kafka let out a loud sigh of relief. The belongings to him did not matter. They could build those again.

"But," said Daena as she lowered her head.

"But what?" Kafka in his regular fashion gurgled his words several times.

"He got one of us," a sturdy voice interrupted. It was Koshti. "There was nothing we could do."

Hearing Koshti's words, Darien's heart opened to a grief he had not felt since he was eight, when his father was about to kidnap him and his sister. He knew what had happened.

Evren had been captured.

Chapter 13
The Reunion of Old Foes

A cardinal compass would point to no specific direction on Ashkhas Island. It bore no east. No west. No north. No south. The short nights and long days were enough evidence to demonstrate the island's unique magnetic deviation. Its azimuth was in a category all by its own. Life struggled to exist on the Tomb's side of the island. It was shriveled and made up of dry foliage with worn out roots and branches, soft white sand aging into slimy moist dirt with creatures just as foul. This was the vortex of an evil empire with diabolic emperors and viziers. And it was here where Fulad Zereh had left a trail of dead shrubs and saplings behind him.

He had reached the entrance of the place he called home, the Zolmkhaneh, which was not far from Hubal's temple. There was a deep shaft with covered earthen barrows that led to an archway. Through the archway was a stone house on an open field with Tavara Hill visible beyond. Evren, who lay still on Fulad's shoulder, had seen that even when peaceful, Fulad had a propensity for destruction. Next to the dead foliage were truncated corpses of little animals Fulad had stepped on to reach his gate. With no chance of escape, Evren had pretended to be unconscious so he wouldn't infuriate his captor. Evren was the long-awaited gift for his mother. Nobody had gotten inside the Golden Circle before. Not even Hubal. Evren and the rest had always been prepared to shift when danger approached. But with the arrival of Darien, the good inhabitants were so concerned there could be a chance it would all end that they failed to remain vigilant the moment Fulad attacked.

Now he stood on the ridge past the archway. This was his mother's place. A long time ago, she reigned supreme, and was charged with leading the attack on the other side of the island. She ruled with complete ruthlessness, eradicating anything and anyone in her way. She was the greatest sorceress Ashkhas Island had seen. They said she was possessed by a demonic spirit, an offspring of Iblis himself. During her reign, the Askhasis were under constant attack. She saw them as a threat and had made it her mission to kill them all. Until one day, Evren was the one to defeat her with a celestial spear known as Shirzad. He spared her life, but the Universe needed to remain in balance. After she was dethroned, the earth cracked open. And out from the ground, from the core of the earth, a place known as Agartha, a new more tactical and formidable adversary emerged. His name was Hubal. He was now the ruler by natural order and Cazi had to swear her allegiance to him. Power is an intoxicating sensation. Ever since she lost hers, vengeance has been the only thing consuming her.

Today was her day of redemption and Evren was to pay it with his life.

Fulad walked towards a pool outside the main house. He tossed Evren onto the ground. Evren knew what to expect. He had not seen Cazi since their epic battle. Evren to this day regretted dethroning her. He had failed to predict what the circumstances would be should he be victorious. He should have known that a throne never sits idle. By getting rid of Cazi, he had opened the gateway for Hubal to enter Ashkhas Island and Hubal was a hundred times more treacherous and fatal than Cazi.

"Get up!" screamed Fulad as he lightly kicked Evren on the ground. "Your sad excuse of existence will soon come to an end old man."

Evren, wearing his permanent narrow smile, didn't seem spooked by Fulad's threatening words. He got back on his feet and dusted off his porcelain-white cloak, now stained with the dirt and mud laying around him. For Evren, words were like little birds that pick insects off the back of rhinoceroses. They never bothered him as his confidence in faith and in himself was as strong and impenetrable as a rhinoceros' skin.

"I'm going to enjoy seeing you suffer for what you did to me and my mother," said Fulad. He poked Evren on the back like a feline playing with its catch before tearing it to pieces.

"Now my boy, be gentle," interrupted Cazi. She was neck-deep in the pool, which, along with water, was filled with thousands upon thousands of snails. She slowly got out of it. The snails had secreted purple dye onto her dress, which was long enough to mop the dirt on the ground. She was a timeless beauty and was as glossy as a stainless steel blade. And as lethal as one.

She walked right up to Evren and said, "It's been a long time Evren."

"It has indeed," replied Evren.

Cazi started to twist the ring on her index finger. She had imagined this moment countless times. She needed to fidget with something to take her mind off the ecstatic rage she was having trouble holding back. And as much as she would've liked to dig her long sharp nails into Evren's chest and rip his heart out, she knew she had to wait. Hubal had implicitly requested for her to refrain from killing him until he saw him first. His exact words were "I want to look through his patronizing eyes and into his soul and let him hear how I'm going to ruin what he has defended for so long. Once I do that, you can rip him apart limb by limb."

She got close to Evren. Close enough that he could taste her smell. "You don't know how much I am going to enjoy watching you bleed," she said as she gently ran her finger down the side of his face.

Evren stayed still. A part of him wanted to stretch back like a string on a bow and slam his head right into her. But Cazi, he knew, was predictable. She wouldn't retaliate. It was Fulad that was chaos waiting to happen.

"That may very well happen, Cazi. But as long as order is restored, what happens to me is of no significance."

"You're right about one thing. Order will be stored,"

Cazi chuckled as she turned to smile at her son. "Hubal will cross the water and he will bring a new order to the world you are so pathetically in love with."

Evren could not argue with what Cazi said. It had happened before. The predecessors to Hubal and Cazi had succeeded in crossing over, but only for brief periods of time.

He also knew that Darien had an impossible task ahead of him. Hubal wasn't like the rest. He had successfully crossed over several times since having sat on the king's throne. His rule stretched over a thousand five hundred years. Where Cazi was hasty during her reign and wanted to first destroy the Golden Circle's protectors and then cross over, Hubal was an astute schemer. He had defeated many who came before Darien and refrained from invading the world, waiting for the right time to strike. And the right time for Hubal meant seeing the world reach a point of total moral corruption. He felt this was what he had been planning and anticipating for over a millennium. Hubal had watched the sins humans had been committing and how they themselves were destroying one another for over a millennium, and they had finally reached the edge of immorality. They themselves had imposed the perfect time for him to invade and draw them completely into a world of lawlessness, misdeeds and evildoing.

"And you know what the best part is?" said Cazi, water dripping over her purple draped dress. "Me and my son are promised our own dominion on the other side as well. We will be kings and queens of our own land!" she continued with a loud laugh. "Now I can't decide whether I will spare you and torture you for an eternity once we succeed or give you the gift of killing you now."

"You do as you want. My fate was sealed from the moment I could speak and neither you nor Hubal can change that," replied Evren.

"As much as my blood boils with rage, I want you to suffer," Cazi replied. "I want you to suffer for as long as I have. Hubal's right. Why kill you when you can watch the world fall beneath our feet. That for you is more agonizing than death."

She had hit a nerve. If it was not for the passive still smile he always wore, she would have known how her last words had provoked fear in Evren. "You forget, Cazi," he said. "Shams has arrived and the skies will come crashing down before we see him fail."

"Fail?" Cazi cheered as she laughed out vociferously.

Fulad chimed in. "That frail little man? I saw him amongst you. I smelt the fear oozing out of his body. He's nothing more than a particle of dust which I will gladly wash off," said Fulad while he wrapped his knuckles with his other hand.

"Look around you, Evren! You're done. And we both know what happened the last time your savior came to the island," said Cazi.

For her, those before Darien had been nothing more than mere chemicals and water wrapped in a body. She despised humans just as much as she did Evren.

Evren put his head down and started to recite hymns.

"Yes" Cazi hissed. "Pray to your God for mercy, for I

135

will show you none and we will afflict unworldly pain to this Shams of yours like we did to your last savior."

Evren's voice cracked yet nothing came out. He prayed history would not repeat itself.

Again.

Chapter 14
Saving Evren

Darien and Kafka heard the tragic news just as the sun was disappearing and the sky filled with bleak clouds and faraway stars.

"But how can that be?" asked Darien frantically. "I thought you said only the Ashkhasis could shift?"

"I did," Kafka replied. "And I did not lie." He hesitated for a minute, and looked at Koshti meaningfully.

"Are you guys going to talk?" shouted Darien, even more furious than before. "There's something you guys aren't telling me, isn't there?"

Darien grabbed a handful of his shirt and fanned himself with it to cool down. He was still sweating from the long run but what he was finding more exhausting were the constant surprises they kept throwing at him. Kafka and Koshti's heads swung like a pair of oscillating pendulums as each tried to indicate to the other that he should speak, but neither wanted to confront Darien.

"Enough damn it!" Darien screamed. "I swear to God! If you guys don't,"

"Fulad is an Ashkhasi!" Kafka finally yelled. He

glared at Koshti, who shrugged his shoulders in response.

"Huh? What do you mean? What do you mean he is an Ashkhasi?" Darien's tone went flat, bafflement subduing his rage.

Kafka grabbed a stick, took a few steps back to find a spot with soft sand, and started to draw a large circle on God's canvas. He then took a breath and, like a preacher beginning his sermon, said, "This is the world as you know it. Everything that makes up this world—you, humans, animals, plants, us, every living creature—resides in this celestial sphere." Finishing the circle, he drew a line right through the middle and dug the stick into the sand on one of the sides. "This is us. Evren told you that we are here to create the balance needed for life to prosper." He then lifted the stick and pointed it to the other half. "What would we bring equilibrium to if the other half didn't exist? We along with Hubal and the rest of his underlings all hail from Agartha, which is the center crux of the earth. There would be no us if it wasn't for them."

Darien felt nauseated and blue in the face. How could both come from the same place? He begun to think perhaps he had been asking the wrong questions. If he could, he would have walked away from it all. He would have jumped right back into the water and hoped it would wash him back to his unjust and imperfect world. His distrust was growing as his patience dwindled, and now he was beginning to think that the Golden Circle's inhabitants weren't as celestial as he had initially thought.

"How can that be?" Darien impatiently asked.

"Gosh I wish Evren was here," sighed Kafka as he

looked up in the dark sky. "I don't know how to tell you this but there is no such thing as a single righteous deed, only a righteous interpretation of a single deed."

"So what are you saying? That if I kill someone and I think it's morally right, then that's fine? That if I steal because I am poor, then it's fine?" questioned Darien. Kafka's words were coming off somewhat indifferent to him, especially considering that he would now be haunted forever by the image of sticking his sword in Ghoul.

"It's not that simple, Darien," interjected Kafka. He knew it would be difficult for Darien to grasp the idea that sin streams from the same fountain that virtue flows.

"It never is," replied Darien. He bent his knees and rested his hands on his legs. "What you're telling me changes everything I have known and felt since I could remember."

Darien had always been an eccentric, a natural autodidact who had developed his own school of thought about life. He knew there was a higher power beyond good and evil. He knew that there is a secret hidden formula to Utopia and it resided in every human being who believed in universal moral principles. And Kafka, from the self-proclaimed defenders of good, was now telling him that, even amongst the Ashkhasi, there was no absolute virtue. Darien's mind began to wander. What assurance did he have that there wasn't a treacherous snake amongst these beings? How was he to know they were not morally bankrupt?

The balls and toes under his leather-skin boots bore all his weight as Darien stared at the perfect geometric shape.

And then it hit him.

Kafka's drawing resembled the Greek letter *Phi,* Φ. Anyone who had spent time on an American university campus or was part of a fraternity or sorority would recognize it immediately. But rather than frat parties, the symbol reminded him of an enigmatic professor whose course he had taken during his freshman year. The course was Physics 101 taught by Professor Garibaldi, who had immigrated to the United States to be part of the US nuclear program team. He had worked with Einstein himself, and must have been over seventy when he taught the class at Boston University. Darien admired and respected everything about Professor Garibaldi. He was as animated as a two-year-old child who had many corky habits. For one, his fashion orientation was not what one expected of a nuclear scientist. He wore fluorescent ties with colorful sneakers to match and a wristwatch with the image of a clown on its face, with stretched-out arms replacing the clock's hands. All of the scientists taught in Professor Garibaldi's class were known as Papas and Mamas. Sir Isaac Newton was Papa Newton. There were Papa Einstein, Papa Galileo, Papa Tesla and even Papa Shams. All of Darien's classmates carried the same honored moniker from Papa Garibaldi as well.

The first thing Papa Garibaldi did when he entered the classroom on the first day wearing a radiant and atomic smile was write on the blackboard, *the day you are born is the day you start dying.* He then turned to face his pupils and said in his high-pitched, thick Italian accent, "If you have gotten this far, then you can read what I have written despite my terrible handwriting. Let me repeat it. The day you are born is the day you start dying. I do not care what you choose to do with your time. If you want to go drinking every night, you can do that. If you want to play video games, you can do that. If you want to sleep in my class, you can do that. And if you want to change the world, you can do that as well. Just remember what I wrote on the board."

"As for me," he continued. "I was a curious boy. I sought answers to questions that nobody in my village could answer for me. So what did I do? I went to university and found my answers in books. But a strange thing happened, the more answers I got, the more questions I asked. I chose Physics as a major and specialized in quantum mechanics when Papa Einstein's paper inspired me. I was a hungry twenty-year-old scholar like you all. But why did I choose physics? Well, physics in Greek means the knowledge of nature and what better subject would give me answers to matter, time and space and my hunger for understanding it all?"

He then turned to the blackboard, wrote "physics" and, right under it, the word *Seek* and the letter *Phi*.

"This is what I seek. I seek the Golden Ratio and at one point in this class, we will get to that."

The Golden Ratio, *1.6180339887...* was an infinite irrational number derived from something known as the Fibonacci sequence, which was named after an Italian mathematician, Leonardo Fibonacci who about eight hundred years ago introduced the Indo-Arabic numerical system to Europe. The Indo-Arabic numerical system was developed by the most outstanding mathematician, where the very word *algorithm* derived from his name. He was a Persian mathematician by the name of Muhammad Al Khwarizmi.

The Fibonacci numbers are a sequence whereby each subsequent number in the sequence was the sum of the previous two numbers. And the golden ratio, also known as *Phi*, was the ratio between each of the consecutive numbers. The ratio could be seen everywhere and in everything. It could be seen in the pyramids of Egypt or the Parthenon in Greece. It could be seen on Da Vinci's immortal painting, on Mona Lisa's face or even in the surreal works of Salvador Dali. It could be heard in music from John Coltrane to Michael Jackson. This ratio was so magical that it could even be used to describe proportions in nature itself, from the smallest atoms to the largest bodies in our universe. It could be seen in leaf arrangements, the bracts of a pinecone, or fish scales— from living cells to a single grain of wheat. Darien had always seen this numinous number as the crossroads where the esoteric world merged with the scientific one. And it was Papa Garibaldi who, in one of his lectures covering these phenomena, said that nature had an innate ability to count on this distinctive proportion to maintain its own balance.

Maintain its own balance Darien thought to himself.

And this is exactly what Kafka's drawing was: *Phi*, the Golden Ratio. Everything Kafka had said suddenly made divine sense as everything occurring in Darien's world as well as on this enchanted island fell into perfect juxtaposition. Everything did come from the same source, the Golden Ratio to which every phenomenon blended. The universe in motion was about to roll its next number. And the result could either be the nefarious realm of Hubal or the better world that Darien and the Circle's inhabitants envisioned. To the Creator, it really did not matter who won, just as long the balance of the Golden Ratio was preserved. Darien now understood what Evren and Kafka had been trying to tell him. He understood why he had those omens as a kid growing up. He had to stop the inimical Hubal.

Darien jumped up as if Papa Newton's apple had just hit his head. "Where did Fulad take Evren? I need to save him. We need to save him."

Darien was immersed in a state of metanoia, calm like a still river but yet burning like a dry log of wood on fire. Still, his moment of enlightenment did not seem to galvanize the others who had begun to gather around Kafka and Koshti. They wore looks of despair. Darien could tell from their silence that they feared even attempting to break into Zolmkhaneh would be suicide. He needed to instill some strength in them.

"Do you believe in the prophecy?" asked Darien as he looked right into the eyes of all of them. Everyone remained silent.

"Do you believe in yourselves?" Darien asked, hoping this might trigger an answer.

Still no response.

Darien placed his hands on his hips and hunched his

shoulders forward. "Guys," he said. "I've never felt or thought clearer than this moment. I have been brought here for one purpose. You serve one purpose. What would we make of ourselves if we did not act right now?"

"Darien," Koshti finally spoke. "It's not that we don't want to do anything. Nobody has gone to Zolmkhaneh or Tavara Hill and come out alive."

"Its suicide!" Kafka screeched.

Their words only got Darien worked up. "But we can beat them!" he said enthusiastically. "We've got a divine decree to succeed. There is too much good in the world to let Hubal or Cazi win."

Kafka raised an eyebrow.

"We've got strength in numbers. We've got the sword of Zulfiqar. And we've got the Almighty who wants us to succeed," continued Darien with eyes wide open and nostrils flaring.

The few Ashkhasis along with Kafka and Koshti who stood in front of Darien were getting fidgety. Darien knew he had their attention now.

"Don't you think Evren would have gone back for you? Don't you think he would've gone to the ends of the universe for any of you?"

"We would do the same Darien, but if we go and do not succeed, then not only will he die along with us, but we will not be able to complete the prophecy," said Kafka.

"Which prophecy would that be?" said Darien.

"Well, just like you have yours, we have ours. And ours is simple. All hundred and fourteen of us have to stand by you when you confront Hubal."

"Damn it you lot, not everything is up to destiny. We have to create our own and saving Evren, one of your companions is more important than any prophecy that exists!" Darien said in astonishment, anticipating they would find it in their hearts that saving Evren was the only thing they should be concerned with. There was no need to mourn, for there was still hope.

Still there was no answer. Darien knew he needed to get to Tavara Hill, not just to rescue Evren but also get the Ayna.

"Fine!" Darien said, tossing his hands in the air. "Then I am going by myself. Just remember, every moment we lose is a moment Hubal gains! Now I don't need any of you to come. Just point the direction to Tavara Hill," he said as he pulled his sword out of his shield's handles.

Kafka stepped forward and leaned on his hind hoof. "Darien, I can't let you do this…" He took a step closer. "I can't let you do this alone. So I will be coming with you."

Darien gently nodded his head at Kafka and gave out a narrow smile similar to Evren's at Kafka's willingness.

"I'm in too."

"Me too."

"Count me in."

"We're coming, Evren."

"I'm in."

The chants of support came from every direction. Darien's heart raced as his eyes and smile widened with every Ashkhasi who volunteered to join Evren's rescue mission. Hearing one Ashkhasi after another chorus in their support invigorated him.

Darien raised his sword and shouted gleefully, "For Evren and for all that is right and just!"

A roaring chant broke out as all raised their hands. Darien looked around and saw the fire in their eyes. The cage had been rattled and he knew any man or woman with a righteous cause had an invincible armor stronger than even Fulad Zereh's magic-coated skin.

"You are all fearless. Now, we don't need to take an army to Zolmkhaneh. Me and Kafka will head to the Hill, but you all need to remain vigilant and prepared for when they attack again," said Darien.

He realized for the first time on how a strong spirit is contagious. It can move mountains. It can turn thoughts into actions. It can even make creatures who are so rigid in their ways bend their beliefs for a worthy cause.

"I need you guys to believe in me and believe in yourself. This moment is mine to fulfill. I will get there and defeat Fulad and bring Evren back. As God is my witness, I will die before I fail," said Darien. He planted his hand on Kafka's shoulder "Are you ready?"

"You were right, there is no way to avoid going to that wretched place. Guess this is as good a time as any, so let's do this," replied Kafka with enthusiasm. He then turned to Koshti and told him to stay alert.

As they ran at a steady pace through the thick green coves, Darien found himself in his own thoughts again. The little drive down memory lane regarding Papa Garibaldi's class made him realize how pitiful the past few months had been. He had been so misguided, so consumed by pity and self-loathing that he forgot what really mattered to him most. And right then and there he decided to take an oath to never take another second for granted. *If I get out of here, I will make every second count*, he thought to himself. He was beginning to build a covenant for life in his mind. And the first lesson was to follow his instincts from now on. If a job didn't feel right, he would quit. If the next girl he dated felt iffy, he would kick her to the curb. From this moment on, he would follow his *heart*, no matter what the consequences. This would be his covenant's first constitution, allow the magic embroidered in his heart to guide him.

"Hold on hold on do you hear that?" said Kafka as he slowed to a halt deep in the heart of the island.

"I don't hear anything," said Darien.

Then the thunderous stomps that Darien had failed to pick up while in thought began to get louder and louder. Darien and Kafka just stood looking at each other. Darien for a moment thought it was Fulad, but this time the trembles were stronger and much more frequent.

"What is that?" Darien asked Kafka.

"Are we in trouble now!" said Kafka shrilly as he rubbed the side of his face with both hands. He grabbed Darien's hand and started pulling him back in the direction from which they had come. "Run," he stuttered.

"Run?" a surprised Darien replied.

"Run! Sarsaoks, run!" yelled Kafka at the top of his lungs.

And Darien saw a stampede blitzing right at them.

They came charging and before Darien could think, he was running behind Kafka. Darien turned and caught a glimpse of the Sarsaoks, big wooly creatures with massive horns that looked like distant relatives of bison. They were gaining on them fast. Kafka, a few steps ahead of Darien, scouted for places to slip between the trees and distance them from these capable and forceful beasts. The Sarsaoks trampled everything in front of them, even the resilient palm trees. In the dark, only trailing both Darien and Kafka by a few feet now, he could see their long horns. Not only were they long and massive but they were made out of pure gold: a poacher's dream come true. The island's very DNA had seemed to permutate and trickle down to a diverse range of creatures that could otherwise only be seen in fabled myths recorded thousands of years ago.

Much to Darien's dismay, Kafka had somehow vanished during the run. He thought he heard Kafka yelling out his name, but it was too late as he had lost him during the ongoing Sarsaok charge.

He knew the island much better than the immigrant and knew the habits of the Sarsaoks so it was not long before he got to a clear area. It would now be impossible to go back and find Darien as the plush green plant kingdom the island served was the most tangled of mazes and it would be long after the end of time before he could find him. He knew his best shot was to head back to the Circle, recruit some of the others and disperse around the area the Sarsaoks charged. He pulled his coin out and the falcon spawned out of it along the lit trail to the Circle.

Kafka ran as though his life depended on it. The Sarsaoks were not expected and Darien alone in these wild woodlands was not a good idea.

Meanwhile, Darien kept on running. He was almost certain Kafka could take care of himself. He was more concerned with his own survival. He ran as fast as his legs would allow him until he reached a patch of dry, peeling trees with thousands upon thousands of parched branches. He thrust himself into the shedding branches for cover.

Then a voice screeched, "Quick, this way!"

Darien squinted into a shadowy passageway through the branches to try and make out who it was, thinking it must be one of the others from the Circle.

But before he could make out the voice, the earth-shattering Sarsaoks were coming right at him again. He leaped through the branches and ran right through the passageway. It was a narrow path, and he had to lean sideways to get through it.

"This way, this way!" the voice whispered in the pitch black.

The voice was calm, its hums that reverberated in Darien's ear sounding like they came from a larynx with only one vocal fold. Darien followed his Piper's low voice. He would thank him once he got through the narrow alleyway fit for a human half his size.

Chapter 15
Meeting Nasnas

The coast cleared and Darien could no longer hear the ear-crushing thuds from the Sarsaoks' destructive parade. He dusted off what leaves remained on him from the parched trees. He could only see a couple of feet ahead in the darkness, but looking beneath his feet he noticed the trail of a single footprint, more than twice the size of Darien's sole, moving forward alongside the print of some object that had been dragged along behind it.

Strange, Darien thought to himself as he caught his breath from his exasperating escape. The single print must be that of the one who had helped him steer to safety. Then he saw him, The footprint had the markings of a big creature as it bore five toes but was more than twice the size of Darien's sole. He looked ahead while pacing his breath so his heartbeat would slow down after the exasperating escape from the big fleece covered beasts.

And there he was, the Ashkhasi who had saved his life. He had found a spot to squat right in front of Darien and was staring right back at Darien with a peering eye.

"You saved my life. I can't possibly thank you

enough," said Darien.

The inhabitant sat there staring back at Darien.

"What's your name?" said Darien.

"My name's Nasnas." The creature got up off the ground turned so that only his profile faced Darien, which Darien found odd.

"Nice to meet you, Nasnas, the name's Darien. I don't think we met earlier." It was more of a question than a comment, although he assume that Nasnas must be from the Circle. If he was one of Hubal's henchmen he would have had his head hanging on a stick by now.

"No we haven't met," he replied, still only showing one side of his face. Darien was not the slightest offended by his impolite body language. After all, Nasnas had just saved his life.

"Well then, Nasnas, once again thank you."

Nasnas then turned towards Darien, the eye that had been facing Darien lit up like a shooting star. What Darien saw would have given him a seizure on any normal day. But being stranded on an island with a man that looks like a goat, another who's facial organs are planted on the palm of his hands and creatures from old Iranian, Arabic and Turkish folklore his grandfather read to didn't make what he saw next strange. Nasnas was literally half of a man, with one arm and one ear on one side and one leg and one eye on the opposite side of a full midsection. The trails he spotted earlier made sense now. Nasnas' long leg and opposing arm, which dragged on the ground, that gave him the ability to balance himself, were what left behind one footprint.

Darien could not remember noticing Nasnas at the Circle earlier, but thinking it impolite to stare he turned away and said, "Right, I'll need to go back and find Kafka."

"Kafka? Kafka? That fool with a tongue as sharp as a blunt knife?" blurted Nasnas while hopping towards Darien.

"I take it you guys are not the best of friends," Darien replied, sheepishly smiling back.

"Friends? Far from it," replied the limping Nasnas.

His tone of resentment was something Darien had not seen since he had arrived. Nasnas reminded him of his colleagues when year-end bonuses were announced at Baraka Capital. The rumor mills would work around the clock with whispered spite similar to that of Nasnas. The other Ashkhasis he had met had a calm aura. Nasnas was different.

"We're not friends" said Nasnas. "He always hides under his pathetic jokes. And the last time I saw him, he would not stop cracking pathetic jokes about my body. It's not my fault I was made this way." His voice was now wrapped in gloom, and as he grunted, his eye filling up with water.

"I know what you mean, he does overdo it sometimes. But I have come to understand he means no harm," replied Darien. He tried hard not to stare at him as Nasnas struggled to balance himself. Darien knew this was just one half of the story. As outlandish as Kafka's jokes may be at times, he did not think Kafka would ever bully any of the others on the island.

"I haven't seen you before," said Nasnas.

Now his turn to present a question more than a comment. Darien paused. If he was an Ashkhasi, wouldn't he have known about Darien's arrival? "Are you not with the rest from the Golden Circle?" he asked.

Nasnas, unable to hold himself back, burst into laughter. "Me? With them? They wouldn't let me in even if I wanted," he said. He grabbed a dry stick from the ground and put the butt of it under his single armpit like a crutch to balance himself. "I am not an Ashkhasi."

Darien was puzzled. He thought all living creatures on the island were Ashkhasis. "What do you mean?"

"I am what you would call a nomad. I am neither from the Circle nor from Hubal's domain. I stand alone. I have this island to call home yet I am homeless. I spend my days being alone as I have no friends. My curse," Nasnas paused. "My *existence* has led me to become an outcast. I have roamed these forests for as long as I remember."

Darien began to feel a tad uneasy. Even though Nasnas did not look physically threatening, Darien's instincts were telling him to be cautious. Darien thought it best to turn back. Finding Kafka and finishing what they had started was the only thing that mattered.

"Well, you can say now that you have one friend on this island. After what you did, I owe you and if you can think of any way I can return the favor, I will promise to do so," said Darien.

"Yes," Nasnas hissed. "I can perhaps think of a thing or two you can do for me."

"Sure, just tell me what it is," replied Darien.

"Well, I will tell you once I have brought you back to Evren and that wretched goat at the Circle."

"Ah! So you know Evren as well?" Darien was glad to hear at least he bore no animosity towards the old man. He couldn't be one of Hubal or Cazi's accomplices or he would have known that Evren had gone missing.

"Yes, I know Evren very well. Allow me to take you back. I know these woods like the back of my hand," said Nasnas as he opened his palm. "That's great, thanks but I best head back and get Kafka with me and help you and him resolve whatever differences you may have," said Darien. He saw no need to share Evren's disappearance with a stranger.

"No!" Nasnas said. He appeared instantly infuriated, but calmed down right away. "There are other dangers in this side of the island and I am sure Kafka has headed back to the Circle. If you turn back through there then I will not be able to help you. Besides, how will I then get what you owe me?"

"Fair enough, then let's head back to the Circle." Darien had grown more weary and suspicious. He turned around to grab his shield and sword which were stuck in between the sharp branches through the tight pathway. "Let me grab my things and we can leave right away."

Then Darien thought he heard Nasnas say something.

"What was that?" Darien turned.

"I didn't say anything," Nasnas replied.

"Ok, I thought I heard you say something." Darien turned back to pull his shield from the sharp thorns that had snagged it on his way through.

"All I ever want is to be whole again," murmured Nasnas.

Darien wasn't hearing voices. He turned to face Nasnas, but the beast clobbered him on the head with all his might. The blow sent Darien crumpling to the moist mud. He was losing consciousness. Through hazy vision he could make out Nasnas standing right on top of him. The strong blow had taken the wind out of Darien's lungs. He was fading further and further away with every passing moment.

Nasnas stopped jabbing him as soon as he saw Darien's eyelids close. He quickly hopped over to a palm tree which was not more than twenty feet away and began to violently rip several of its sharp leaves. Nasnas pulled on the leaves so hard that stamens dispersed and filled the air around him. He then tore out a few strings of vines from the same palm tree's trunk and started to wrap them on both ends of the perfectly placed leaves that lay on the ground. The half finished product was a sled which he dragged back to the spot Darien remained unconscious.

He lifted Darien with the one arm he had and rolled him over on to the leaves. His swift yet vehement craftsmanship had him short on breath.

He was breathing heavy while smiling and looking right down on Darien as he turned and said, "And this is how you are going to pay me back."

Chapter 16
Darien & Hubal

Nasnas had dragged Darien's unconscious body all the way to the Tomb on a makeshift sled. With the help of a pair of Hubal's soldiers, he strapped Darien into a torture chamber that lay underneath the stairway Kayret had earlier climbed. A pair of golden gyves mounted on the limestone rocks on the ground shackled Darien's feet. His hands were fitted tight in a pair of golden manacles secured by a hook to the wall. The chains stretched his arms out to either side. Nanas had now delivered the anointed one right into Hubal's bleak golden hand.

"Good work, Nasnas. For this you will have what so long you have longed for," said Hubal as he stood in front of the catatonic Darien.

"I will be forever grateful Your Excellency," said Nasnas, unable to hold back an exuberated smile.

He now could have the whole body he had always wished for. Cazi could have fulfilled his dream a long time ago, but Nasnas had always been fearful of going to Tavara Hill and confronting the sorceress and her unpredictable son. He had known with Hubal's blessings she would not be able to turn him down. This was his retribution and he was going to see it through.

"Kayret!" yelled Hubal.

Kayret came running at the speed of sound as Hubal's loud voice could even wake up the sun.

"Yes. Yes Your Majesty," said Kayret, his knees buckling.

"We are on the right path. You can go to Cazi and tell her to come here with Fulad," instructed Hubal.

"Yes Your Majesty," a quivering Kayret replied.

"And tell that old hag that she can do whatever she wants with the old man. He is no longer needed. Our mission is to begin. Theirs is about to end," said Hubal as he made a fist with his golden hand.

Kayret nodded his head, walking backwards so as to not turn his back on Hubal. As soon as he reached the door, he dashed out to follow Hubal's instructions.

"Your Excellency," interjected Nasnas. "Will Cazi do what you have promised?" Nasnas was worried as Hubal had not included his promise to Kayret as part of his message.

Hubal went silent. His eyes fixed on Nasnas. "Are you questioning my word?" he said gently.

"No! No, I would never!" Nasnas replied, now trembling with fear.

"What I say is. When I say you will get what you want, then so it shall be," said Hubal. "Now, where are his belongings?" continued Hubal changing the subject altogether.

"Belongings? What?" Nasnas was thrown off.

"His shield. His sword, the sword of Zulfiqar! I want to stick his sword through his own heart. Where is it?"

Nasnas realized he left them back by the parched plants, but it was too late. He had been so excited to get to this juncture he forgot to pick them up. Nasnas began to palpitate. There was no room for mistakes with Hubal. His fury was beyond measure. And now he was scared that not only would he not get his other half, he would lose what he already had.

"I...I...I forgot to pick them up," said Nasnas while his shivering leg sent murmurs across the cold stone tiles. Much to his surprise, Hubal showed no reaction or rage. He just stood there and looked at the manacles Darien was chained to.

"Well then, you need to go get it," said Hubal calmly.

Nasnas' eye lit up, "I will run there immediately!"

"And make sure you are back in time or you will remain like this for eternity," said Hubal.

Nasnas grabbed his cane, which had been resting on the wall, and began to march as fast as he could back to the spot he had clobbered Darien on the head.

Φ

Darien was slow to come to his senses. Eyes slanted and head spinning, he had no idea what had transpired. He heard a squeak echo, perhaps the sound of a door. With his eyes half shut, he could see light entering from somewhere and reflecting off something golden. Darien's chin rested on the soft cotton thread weaved on his coat.

He slowly lifted his chin from the woven cotton thread and saw a silent figure in front of him, but his blurry vision started to fade as he moaned again.

Darien felt the frigid brass gyves chained on his hand and legs. The golden metal sent neurons rocketing through his spine, jolting him right out of his slumber. Seeing now his shackled limbs, he tried to muscle out of them. Darien tussled with the chains, only to give up after several attempts. He let out a loud cry.

Hubal laughed out loud at Darien's attempt at freedom, and Darien realized he had been face to face with him the whole time. Darien could feel the evil that wreaked out of Hubal and his golden hand that shined radiantly as he stood in a ruby red robe hung by a collar that stretched down to his sternum. Darien could see a matching gold medallion flashing on his large dark chest.

Darien wrestled with the chains a little more but to no avail.

"And you're Evren's savior," said Hubal as he raised his eyebrow and grinned. "He expects you to save humanity? You can't even get out of a few chains."

Darien bit his lower lip. The friction between his skin and the shackles made Darien angrier. He was mad for not being cautious enough. He had let his carelessness get the better of his instincts. And now he was locked up, enraged by Nasnas and his betrayal.

Nothing comes without a price, he thought to himself. The notion of complete selflessness was a lost virtue. Kafka and the rest in the Golden Circle still bore this noble trait, but it had somehow died with humankind and every other of the earth's creatures. Darien wrestled a little more with the manacles, hoping by some miracle the welded cuffs would break.

"You are not going anywhere." Hubal's deep voice interrupted Darien and his attempt to break free. "I have plans for you."

Darien grew tired from the tug of war he was playing with his chains.

"You better save your energy, for you are going to need all that you can muster," said Hubal.

Breathing heavily and still a bit dizzy from the thud on his head, Darien looked right at Hubal and shrieked, "What have you done with Evren? What have you done with him?"

"Petty, petty, petty," answered Hubal as he took two steps closer to Darien. "He is soon to be relinquished of his soul." He tilted his head sideways as he looked at Darien. He was surprised by Darien being more concerned about Evren's wellbeing when he was about to let out his own last breath.

"There is something familiar about you. What last name do you go by?"

Darien gave him no reply.

"Well," Hubal continued. "It does not matter any longer for it is time for darkness to shine. As for the old man, his fate now lies in Cazi's hands and I know she will not go lightly on him."

Darien started to fume. He could feel Hubal's commanding presence and how calm he was. His right hand, which looked like it was smelted in gold, had a mesmerizing effect. But if it had not been for the chains, he would've reached for Hubal's throat.

"I can't wait to stand over your dead corpse when words run out and they no longer fill up space," he said.

His words sent Hubal into a humorous frenzy. The frequencies from his laughter shook the shackles, as he walked towards a small window from which moonlight entered the small dingy chamber. "Tell me, do you know how pearls are made?"

Again Darien refused to entertain his question.

"A pearl sits idle and quiet inside the shell of an oyster dug within the dark depths of the sea. It grows in the absence of light. It stays down at the bottom of darkness for months and even years until some human brings it out on the surface and opens its shells and there is this hard, beautiful and spellbinding gem that your kind are desperate enough to display on the places where their hearts and ears rest." Hubal paused for a moment to walk back towards Darien. "That is what I am. I am the pearl your world will adorn and worship. I have been living in the shadows for millennia and now that your world is on the cusp of its own destruction, I will cross the island and rule over the demise of your men and women." Hubal's words were getting under Darien's skin as he tussled with the chains once more.

"See, I have been to your side. I have whispered in the ears of some of the men that roamed the earth, but what they have done is insignificant to what I am capable of. And soon, all of the loved ones you have left behind will feel my wrath. They will either have to obey me or suffer a pain worse than hell's wrath. By the time I am through, death for humans will be a luxury."

Hubal's words sent a shiver down Darien's spine as his thoughts rushed to his mother and sister. The faces of his family, friends and even those who had hurt him clouded his mind like a Scottish winter's day. But most of all, it was the two women in his life that he could not bear seeing anything happen to. Hubal's threatening words pushed Darien into a ferocious vigor. He could feel his blood boiling under his skin. His thighs started to stiffen, the veins on his shoulder and arms pulsating on his skin.

"As God is my witness, I will bury hell itself before I let you do anything to my world." Darien was now gushing with a wrath of his own. "And if it is not me, then God Himself will strike you down."

The mere thought of the world he knew ending lit up Darien's eyes as he found himself the recipient of his second constitution in his life's covenant: the constitution of his *world* and its preservation. He would swear to protect it at all costs. He would always see more good than evil in it and strive to fight for his world.

Hubal seemed no longer amused. "You keep bringing up God's name," he said in an inquisitive yet placid tone.

"In the world of kings and peasants, the one who holds power knows the truth. The truth lies with the king." Hubal leaned his face close enough for Darien to feel his breath.

"And I am king," he muttered while grabbing Darien by his long hair. "You on the other hand look like a peasant. You smell like a peasant. You talk like a peasant.

And you believe in God as a peasant does. He is nothing more than an illusion to make you believe you matter."

Darien thrust his neck back as he growled, so enraged that his own saliva gushed out of his mouth like a dog with rabies.

Hubal let his hair go as he saw Darien's eyes percolate with blood under his indigo irises. "Tell me, what is your name?"

"You will know my name when I send you back to God, you miserable fiend."

Hubal smiled. He could use someone with Darien's fierceness.

"Do you want to learn everything there is about Him? Do you want to learn something about your God?" said Hubal as he took a couple of steps back.

"I know what He needs me to know," said Darien, grinding his teeth.

"People are futile by nature. You are built on nothing more than fickle thoughts. Let me open your eyes for you and show you how you have been misled. You are fortunate to have met me because I know everything there is about Him." Hubal paused for a moment and began to play with the medallion hanging on his chest. "You can now swear your allegiance to me and know everything I know. Have you not learnt that the best way to learn about someone is to befriend their enemy?"

Darien did not answer but kept his glare fixed on Hubal as his chest cavity rose and fell with every breath he took.

"Where has your God been? Where had He been

when immorality corrupted your people?" asked Hubal.

These questions had haunted Darien at certain moments of his life. Whenever he turned on the television and saw the atrocities taking place, these questions would haunt him. When his own father and fiancé had been capable of deceiving him, he asked himself the difficult questions.

"What world is this that you want to protect? Jews, Christians, Muslims—all killing one another in the name of God," continued Hubal, squinting at the names of the religions. "Even Buddhists and Hindus have left a trail of religious blood. God left you alone the moment life in the world you know was created. And a village with peasants needs a king. He who has deserted you from the very beginning is no king."

Hubal paused momentarily, eyes narrowed, his voice oozing with conviction.

"I will bring order. I will take away your moral anarchy. And I will give your people a God worth sitting on the throne," said Hubal as he now raised his hands above his head. "And to God, I will prove to Him that I am just as omnipotent as he is."

Darien started thinking of his younger days. When he was a child, love and compassion came in their purest form. It was inherent in people of all ethnicities, creed and age. He always felt it and knew it existed. The world he knew was a beautiful place. It was a direct reflection of God Himself. But he could not help but consider what Hubal said. *How did we get here?* Darien thought to himself. Now completely helpless, he could not but for the first time begin to lose hope. His eyes started to tear as the thought of not seeing his mother or sister tore his heart into two. He put his head down and began to mumble two words under his breath.

Hubal could hear them.

"Hahaha, yes pray. Pray to God for that is all that's left for you" said Hubal.

Outside, the short night on Ashkhas Island was coming to an end. Darien knew he could not foretell the future but if this is his end, then so be it. And if he were to die, he would air out a fury of words like a descending comet and at least try to extinguish Hubal's flaming ego.

"You claim to know all, yet don't know anything. Here is something I will teach you," said Darien. He grimaced as every cell in his body gathered force and he braced himself to speak. "This is not how it is destined to end. You are not our legacy. You are right about one thing. You are a pearl and you will end up where you belong, deep in the pit of darkness."

"That's where you're wrong. God does not care about which side is bigger, so as long as the Golden Ratio is preserved," a slowly riled Hubal replied. Darien had hit a sensitive nerve. Hubal's hand started to light up as he grabbed Darien by the throat, choking him almost to death as the monster's lips touched his ear. "God will not save you. But I can. I will give you the chance to be my first convert."

Hubal could not make out what Darien was saying as he gasped for air through his crushing windpipe. He let him go.

"I will give you time. But when I march forward, you will have one of two options. Either stand under my shadow or die and rot into the same mud you were made of." Hubal then left the room.

Darien broke down. The chains were the only thing that held him up. Could Hubal have been right? Where was God now that he so desperately needed Him? Darien's short time on Ashkhas Island was becoming nothing more than an endless series of events raising increasingly more difficult questions. Left alone once again, he felt like he was back in his room, chained to his bed with no desire to move.

There was no tomorrow to wake up to.

ظ

Chapter 17
Saving Darien

Kafka's light brown fur was wet, his sweat pores having opened wide from his intrepid Sarsaok escape. He had left a trail of blood behind, running so fast through the woodlands that unexpected thorns and branches had cut deep around his hooves and ankles. He was now standing on the steps of a terrace made out of sedimentary rocks that had taken thousands of years to form. Scattered all around him were mineral hot springs that gushed with warm water and smoke. The Sarsaok were not agile enough to climb these steps so he knew he was in the clear. After dusting himself off and wiping the blood from his hooves with dead leaves he started off in the same direction he had come from, ignoring the trail that was lit from the coin which pointed across the steps towards the Golden Circle. Kafka was tensing up. He needed to get back to where the pandemonium took place. Not only had Evren been taken hostage, but Darien could have very likely met the same doom. He needed to get Darien.

He swiftly got back to the place where they had separated. Looking around, he noticed the shattered broken branches of a thorny labyrinth. Making his way meticulously through it, he saw Darien's sword and shield lying on the ground. His heart started to pound uncontrollably, his legs started giving out on him, and migraines stronger than a Sarsaok stampede pounded through his head. He dropped to his knees and covered his face with his hands. He knew Darien was captured. This was not the way it was supposed to end. He started to gurgle, on the cusp of breaking into tears. But he was interrupted from a sound not too far away. He lifted his head like a radar to hear better. *It could be Darien!* he thought to himself. Or at least he hoped so. Bushes just a few feet ahead of him started to ruffle and a lisped nagging moan aired right behind them. He got right back up and picked up Darien's belongings. This was not Darien's voice. He was all too familiar with the gasping fret. It was Nasnas. As quickly as his sweat-drenched body allowed him, he jumped behind a tree.

Nasnas limped in and started to relentlessly look around, tossing leaves and stones.

"It can't be!" Nasnas screeched even louder. Having lived a life of solitude, he had no one else but himself to talk to on this vast and enraptured island. "What will I do now? How will I tell Hubal I lost them? It must be that wretched goat. He must have come back!" said Nasnas as he punched himself in the head with the only hand he had. He was desperate and his carelessness now could potentially cost him a whole body he had desired his whole life. He had to devise a plan quick for there was no way he could head back without the sword. Hubal was not generous. Two mishaps is one too many with the evil overlord.

Nasnas looked up in the sky, yelling out like a madman out of desperation. The adrenaline exodus calmed him down and he quickly started to devise his own diabolic plan. He knew how proud and arrogant the mother and son were. He could march to Zolmkhaneh and get under Fulad's impenetrable skin by saying that he spied on Kafka. He would tell him that he heard Kafka say now that he was in possession of the Zulfiqar, he could cut Fulad into pieces quicker than a Datom could cut a Dhub. This he thought would light a fire under the hubristic Fulad and he would very well attack the Circle again. It was the only chance he had at getting into the Circle and taking the sword back to Hubal. He wasted no time and started to gallop with one leg and one arm in the direction of the Zolmkhaneh at Tavara Hill.

Kafka, still under cover behind the tree, felt a sharp tap on his back. "My God, Koshti! You scared the living life out of me!" he said as loud as a whisper would allow.

"We got worried. Sarsaoks came storming through and we had to shift," replied Koshti.

Kafka was relieved to see a familiar face, but still startled from the way Koshti had snuck up behind him.

"Where's Darien?" asked Koshti, scanning the vicinity.

"I lost him. We fell right in the middle of the stampede," replied Kafka as he bent his head towards the ground.

Koshti let out a deep sigh. Both Ashkhasis knew what

this meant.

Kafka lifted the sword of Zulfiqar. He could see his own reflection in the flawless blade. Suddenly, Darien's voice was echoing in his head: *We have strength in numbers. We have the sword of Zulfiqar and we've got the Almighty who wants us to succeed.* The words gave Kafka a jolt. He knew he had to do something. The first to follow was just as important as a leader. This was his time to rise to the occasion and do something.

"We have got to save Darien. There is nothing else more important at this moment," he told Koshti.

"But, we don't know where he is," a puzzled Koshti replied. "I do. And we have to do whatever it takes to get Darien to Tavara Hill" said Kafka. Kafka knew from eavesdropping on Nasnas that he had taken Darien to the Tomb. He was not going to let fear consume him, even though none of the Ashkhasis from the Circle had ever seen it except for Evren.

Koshti was aware that Hubal's infamous three hundred and sixty soldiers known as the Yanissaries were always at the Tomb. They were Ashkhas Island's mongrels. Outcast in every universe as well as the hereafter, they found refuge under Hubal's tutelage, who had spent the better part of the millennium training them to become ruthless killing machines. But what was most frightening about the Yanissaries was that death simply did not apply to them. They had no souls, and so could never be killed.

But Koshti was a warrior, and had never shied away from battle. His first impulse revealed a soldier's confidence and discipline as he clenched his fists and said,

"Then by God's grace we will give them hell."

"I'll go with a small team over. You need to stay back and protect the rest just in case anything happens," said Kafka. "But we need to head to the Circle first."

"Ok, we're not far from here. Let's go!"

Φ

Koshti led Kafka until they reached the Circle. Everyone noticed Darien missing. Some sighed, others wore dejected yet dignified faces. Kafka wasted no time. He let the first pack form a mob around him know what had happened.

"Darien has gone missing and we need to act now. I will need two of you to come with me," said Kafka.

He heard no objections. It seemed everyone at the Circle knew what was at stake.

"So who will go with you, Kafka?" said one of the voices from the crowd.

"Ok, our task to save Darien will require a whole lot of stealth and a whole little of size" said Kafka, putting shield and sword on the ground to illustrate his words. "Where are Zamboor and Marmoolak?"

"I'm here, Kafka," a hovering little body buzzed from the crowd.

It was Zamboor. She was tiny enough to fit through a keyhole, but had a long tongue that would flap at such a brisk pace when she spoke that her words reverberated loudly.

"And where's Marmoolak?" said Kafka.

A head from the crowd stretched out like a periscope

on a submarine. "I'm here too, Kafka," Marmoolak said. His seven green eyes, situated all around his head and so large that from far it looked as if he was wearing a crown with big emeralds, gave him the best periphery vision on the island.

"Zamboor, Marmoolak, are you guys ready?" an ecstatic Kafka said.

"Just go ahead and lead the way!" replied Zamboor as she buzzed around Kafka's head. "Let's do this," Marmoolak cheered.

"You guys best get a move on because time is out of our control," said Koshti.

The three headed out. As they quietly hurried to the entrance of the Tomb, Marmoolak with his long neck was able to scout the whole vicinity.

"I can't see any of the Yanissaries," said Marmoolak, his head looming like a lighthouse above them.

"No Yanissaries? That should make things easier. I'll go in with Zamboor. Marmoolak, you stay out here. If you see any sign of the soldiers or Hubal, just yell it out," said Kafka.

Kafka needed to act off of impulse and devise the perfect plan to save the anointed one.

Φ

At the wooden entrance door, Zamboor buzzed right through the keyhole. Once inside there were two soldiers standing guard by the chamber Darien was locked in. She had a hunch he was captive behind the door, as she thought why else would there be soldiers guarding it. She dashed right past them but they had no idea it was Zamboor. To their naked eye, she looked like nothing more than a tiny insect. Once through the chamber, she laid her eyes on a broken and worn-down Darien. She could tell he was deflated, hopeless and chained up helplessly with his head hanging like a tree bearing fruit. She went and landed right on the top of his left ear. Darien had gone so numb that he did not even twitch.

"Darien, before you say anything, I am Zamboor and I am here with Kafka to get you out," she said. Darien sprung his head back and looked over his left shoulder but did not see anyone. It was until Zamboor started flying in front of his eyes that he saw her. He was overwhelmed with joy. Hope had found her way once again. He abided by her request and nodded his head. "Ok there are two soldiers outside. We will have to distract them. You stay tight and we will be back to get you out of here," she said while floating around him with her long red tongue.

This was the closest anyone from the Golden Circle had gotten to the Tomb. And it was finally dawning on Kafka, as he waited outside, that if Hubal or any of the Yanissaries spotted them, it would be off with their heads right then and there. But before he could feed his demon of fear, Zamboor came flying back out.

"There are a couple of soldiers standing guard in front of the chamber where they are keeping Darien. We will need to get them away from the door," she hummed.

"How was he?" Kafka said, unable to mask his concern for Darien.

"He was chained up, but in good spirits as soon as I introduced myself," she replied.

Kafka was relieved to hear that he was still in one piece. The more pressing matter was how to get him out. He needed a moment to think. Before he could draw up a plan, Marmoolak had joined them.

"I spotted the rest. I spotted Hubal. I spotted them all!" a worked-up Marmoolak said. Having seen Hubal had so mortified him that he was trembling and his head was beginning to bob and weave.

"Relax. Where are they?" said Kafka as he placed his hand on Marmoolak's shoulder.

"They are far. They are beyond the Attah hill range," Marmoolak replied. He pointed to a series of tiny hills surrounding an open plain of green algae, a result of a stream from the sea that now had been blockaded by Hubal's army and had dried up. "They are suiting up for battle. They're all getting ready for the invasion."

They were pressed for time. Kafka needed to act.

"Alright, this is the plan. Zamboor, can you go back in and open the locks?" asked Kafka.

"Not the door, it's sealed with a Zolotoy lock," she replied.

The Zolotoy locks were potion-filled safes built by Cazi herself. If by any chance anyone was able to crack the unbreakable code and open them, an alarm system would trigger the ear-deafening scream of a woman and alert everybody within an eight-mile radius.

"Then the only way to get through the door will be to break it without tampering with the lock," Kafka said.

"But Darien's chains, those should be a breeze," said Zamboor, determined to share some positive news as well.

"Marmoolak," said Kafka. "You will need to run, run as fast as you can to create a diversion. They will most likely chase you until a certain point, give up, and then return. That should give us enough time to get Darien out." He saw fear in Marmoolak's eyes, but hoped for the sake of all of them that he would go along with his improvised plan.

"Ok Kafka, how do you want to go about it?" said Marmoolak, much to Kafka's relief. The Ashkhasis rose to the occasion when it mattered most.

"Alright, you'll just need to open the door and let them see you. As soon as you see them charge, make a run for it," Kafka said. "And Zamboor. You go in now, set Darien free and head back to the Circle. I will take him from here."

"Do you not want me to stick around?" a loyal Zamboor hummed.

"No, you need to be with the rest. Remember, strength in numbers," Kafka replied with a smile. "Alright guys, this is for Darien, Evren and everybody else. Let's stay strong and remain alert."

Kafka made his way around the Tomb and hid with his back planted on the cold boulders of the temple while Zamboor flew back in. Meanwhile, Marmoolak tiptoed to the door and gently opened them. The startled soldiers, seeing a long-necked intruder, immediately mounted their swords by their sides and jumped forward towards Marmoolak. As he began to run back into the thick jungle, the two Yanissaries gave chase and disappeared into the thick woodlands. Kafka's plan had worked out flawlessly.

With the soldiers gone, Kafka ran back towards the entrance and stepped into the Tomb. He instantly felt trapped. Aside from the vile stench of carcasses, the Tomb had an unpleasant aura that made Kafka feel boxed in. As he reached the door, Zamboor flew out of the keyhole.

"I've opened the chains Kafka, you sure you don't need me here?" she said, buzzing in circular motions.

"It's ok Zamboor, just head back, I've got it from here," he replied.

Zamboor then floated her way out of the room and back to the Circle.

Kafka pressed his head close to the door. "Darien, Darien! Can you hear me?"

"Boy, am I glad to hear your voice!" Darien's voice came from within.

"Me too, look…" said Kafka. He paused, knowing that he needed to get Darien out at any cost and what he was about to do next meant swallowing his dignity and doing something he had vouched to never ever do. "Look, what I am about to do, I need you to tell me before you're out that you will not tell anyone about," said Kafka while tapping his hoof steadily on the dark cobbles.

"Ok, I won't. Just get me out!" Darien replied.

"Seriously, Darien! Forget about Hubal, if you tell anyone, I will personally chop your head off," said Kafka.

"I promise, Kafka. I promise," replied Darien.

For Kafka, a word of promise was as golden as the sun itself. He was relieved to hear Darien give his word.

"Ok then, I need you take a few steps back from the door."

Kafka placed the sword and shield he had carried with him to the side of the door, taking deep breaths like he was bracing himself to dive underwater.

"Ok here it goes!"

Φ

Darien heard a quaking bang on the door. Then another. And then another.

Next thing he knew, Kafka's head had cracked right through the middle of the thick wooden door. He pulled back out and gave the door one final blow, bursting it into a barrage of tiny little splinters. Darien, relieved to see him, noticed the creature coming into the chamber was having trouble keeping his balance, and grabbed Kafka by the shoulder.

"I thought those things were just a fashion accessory," he said, pointing his head towards Kafka's horns.

"We each have our gifts," said Kafka, stumbling across the floor with his head still spinning. "Mine just happen to be pretty and useful." They both laughed, a result of uncontrollable adrenaline, as Darien ushered him close to a wall so he could sit down until he got his legs balanced under him. But remembering Hubal's sinister face, and imagining what he was capable of doing to humanity and his loved ones, made Darien's blood boil anew quicker than steel on a hot summer's day in Dubai.

The series of events that led to this point flipped his mood faster than a blink of an eye. In a span of a few minutes, he had been beat down, uplifted, humored and now enraged.

"We need to go back and end this as quickly as you are able," Darien said. "Hubal has sent someone to tell Cazi to do whatever she wants with Evren. I looked into the monster's eyes and saw what you meant. I saw nothing but death and pain."

"I have never seen him, but I have seen what he is capable of and that was more than enough for me," replied Kafka.

"Will you manage to walk?" asked Darien as he let go of Kafka's hand to see whether he had his balance back.

"Yes. But this time, let's stay close," Kafka said. He did not want another stampede or the many surprises the island wore to separate them again.

"Let's move then," said Darien as he retrieved his sword and shield. On their way out of the Tomb, he turned and took one last glance at the azoic palace. It only fueled his desire to stick his sword right into Hubal's heart.

Kafka knew how to get to Tavara Hill. He told Darien that he knew Cazi and Fulad lived alone and that no other predator dared to get close to the Hill. Darien said that he had never understood why Cazi never used the Zomorod Box herself to call on Alicanto to defeat Hubal. Kafka was quick to remind him that only a son or daughter of Adam was able to call on the powerful bird. With short sporadic conversations and light feet they got to the base of the Hill, where Darien saw the entrance to Zolmkhaneh.

They heard noises. Somebody was close by, and Darien was no longer going to run. It was time to face the Ashkhasi demons. He gripped tight onto his sword and recited a prayer for the one he was about to slay. Without giving a notice to Kafka he ran towards the direction where they heard the shuffling of leaves. As he got closer he saw that it was Nasnas, and he pounced on him like a lion on a gazelle. Nasnas flew into the air and landed hard on his back. Darien charged him and pointed his sword right under his neck.

Nasnas's eye turned to glass, his pleas to stop appearing to fall on deaf ears as Darien raised his sword over him. He froze, bracing himself for justice to be served. But right before Darien was about to bring his sword down like a guillotine, he looked right into the eye of Nasnas and felt guilty. This creature had suffered enough. His resentment and agony were spawned from his weakness. Some find light in darkness while others let it consume them, and Nasnas happened to be a victim of the latter. Nasnas though did not know what forgiveness was so he planted his face onto his hand waiting to meet his own demise.

"I'm not going to kill you," said Darien, lowering his sword. "I will let you live, but only because I know what you have been through."

"All I wanted was to be whole," said Nasnas as he broke down and started to cry, incapable of understanding how Darien could spare his life.

For Darien, that was all the clemency he would give. "Even if you were whole, you'd still have an empty heart.

Now leave, this is no place for you to be," Darien said.

Nasnas got up and limped away until he was no longer seen. "Don't you think you went a little hard on him?" said Kafka.

"Hard would've been letting him watch me cut his last limbs off. I did what was right," he replied.

"It was. What did you tell him that had him crying like a little infant?"

"I told him the truth."

Kafka then paused. "Darien, are you ok?"

"Yeah why wouldn't I be? I've never felt better," said Darien.

He jiggled his weapons casually to shake off some of the tension building up. But he sensed that Kafka had seen in his rage a side of Darien he had not seen before, and wanted to ask him about what happened back in the torture chamber. Kafka's curiosity though would have to wait. More pressing matters awaited them: the moment had come to call on Alicanto and send Hubal to the abyss he came from. But before he got his hands on the Ayna, there was one thing he needed to do first.

"Now," said Darien as he looked beyond the archways of the Zolmkhaneh. "Let's go free Evren."

ع

Chapter 18
The Battle of Tavara Hill

Luck is the devil with a halo: sometimes she favors the good; other times she favors the bad. But her mercilessness and capricious ways are built on a zero sum game. One's good luck only spells badly for the opposing force. And the good luck which was bestowed on Darien and the denizens of the Golden Circle was to be the misfortune of Kayret.

Darien and Kafka had spotted him passed out on top of a bed of bones of Dhubs. Kayret's luck had led him to come across a tribe of Dhubs right next to the entrance of Zolmkhaneh. It was too good of an opportunity to pass so he devoured every last one of them until he had no more space in his bloated belly. With his gluttonous indulgence, he could no longer stand on his feet and fell deep into a food coma.

He no longer posed a threat to Darien and Kafka on his bed of reptilian cartilages, and the two walked right past him to the entrance of Zolmkhaneh.

Even with luck on their side, Kafka appeared nervous. "I don't know if this is such a good idea, Darien."

Darien on the other hand was as calm as nature's whisper. He paused and turned to face Kafka. "I know what you mean, but we have to be strong. Courage is not the absence of fear, but knowing fear exists and still moving forward. Even if the skies fall down today, we will still not get down on our knees." He wanted to inspire Kafka by quoting one of Persia's immortal kings, Cyrus the Great. If his actions were not going to instill courage, then he hoped the old king's words would succeed where he could not.

"I've heard those words before," replied Kafka while he nodded his head with closed eyes. "A long time ago, but I cannot place who uttered them."

That can't be, Darien thought to himself. Could Cyrus have been one of the anointed ones? How else would Kafka know that Darien had taken his words of inspiration from him?

"We are going to get through this, Kafka. I'm afraid too," lied Darien. "I'm afraid of failure itself. We ourselves do not matter, but if we don't succeed, then a lot of people will pay the price."

Kafka realized there is no turning back and he had taken an oath to be by Darien's side. He also thought about Evren and how he put his own life in jeopardy for everyone's safety. "Alright Darien, I guess this is the moment we fulfill our prophecy," he said with a spur of energy.

But Darien, in now typical fashion, had a sudden change of heart. He only needed to be shown the entrance to Tavara Hill, and Kafka had kept his word by bringing him to its doorsteps. From this point on, he could not keep himself safe, let alone anybody else. He knew from what he had seen of Fulad at the Circle that an extra pair of hands and eyes would increase his chance of succeeding, but his friend had gone above the call of duty to bring him here. He would have him released so that he could go and join the rest of his brethren at the Golden Circle.

"Kafka, you don't need to come any further. You've shown more heart than anyone I've known."

"What? And miss out on all the glory? Not a chance!" He had, in typical Kafka fashion, once again lightened the thick smog of fear around them with his wit. "There is no way you are going in there alone. I told you I would get you to Zolmkhaneh, but I didn't say I wouldn't come in with you. I'm with you all to the end, Adam's son."

Before going through the entrance, Darien closed his eyes, held on tight to his weapons and started to take deep breaths. The showdown with Fulad Zereh and Cazi was about to ensue. He felt the air fill up his lungs. And with every breath that exited his body, he grew stronger. When he opened his eyes, he was ready to confront the evil past the gates.

Entering, they stood in front of the hanging windows outside the Zolmkhaneh. Neither Cazi nor her son was in sight. A carved out dome lay in an open field, where a shimmering light was glimmering. Darien knew there was only one object large and bright enough to give off that glistening light. It was Fulad, and from far he looked exactly like the orb that had sat idle for so long on Edward

Moroni's desk.

Darien looked at Kafka and said, "I'm going for Fulad. You go back inside the Zolmkhaneh and see if you can find Evren."

"But Darien,"

"Just go," Darien softly interrupted him. This was his and only his battle to face.

Kafka looked up and sang a prayer for Darien before making his way to the spiraling turret attached to the rest of the mansion that was coated with soot and cold stones where Evren would have to be somewhere.

Darien took his time walking through the arch and toward the field, his eyes narrowing with every step as he locked them on Fulad. His sword gently grazed the uneven cobblestones under his feet. Darien wanted Fulad to know he was coming. He wanted to face this demon eye to eye. But it wasn't the rasping of Darien's sword that alerted Fulad, who was polishing his own sword on a big rock with his back turned. It was Darien's scent that let Fulad know he had arrived, a scent all too foreign to Fulad to belong to any other than the Golden Circle's paladin.

"You have guts, I will honor you that," said Fulad, his voice as coarse as the booming growls Darien had heard when Fulad attacked the Circle.

Darien was now standing just a few yards away. "You know why I'm here," said Darien clearly and strongly.

Fulad let out a chuckle.

"One of us is going to the afterlife, and one of us is going to stay behind," Darien went on.

"Is that so?" Fulad said with a smirk.

"It is. And I can swear on an eternity in hell that it won't be me leaving."

Darien lowered his eyebrows and his chin as he held out his shield and sword at the hips. The look of amusement on Fulad's face was short lived. He looked right into Darien's sky blue eyes as the sun's light ricocheted off his skin and into them. To his surprise, he saw Darien carrying the sword of Zulfiqar. Nobody had got their hands on it until now.

"You think you and that little piece of metal are going to stop me?" said Fulad, his voice fueled with anger.

Darien looked up momentarily at the magnificent sun above. She was shining right through his skin and into his very soul. Turning back to Fulad, he said, "Yes, for the golden sun rises today and you shall feel her divine burn."

Quicker than he could roar Fulad was charging right at Darien, who remained heedful and prepared. His entire body weight was leaning on his right foot a step ahead of his left. He held his ground, knowing that he would not be able to outpace Fulad. He would have to outsmart and outmaneuver the overgrown fiend.

As Fulad got close Darien pivoted his foot like a master matador and dodged the creature's charge. He was waiting for the right opportunity to present himself so that he could swing the sword and cut through his impenetrable skin. Fulad turned and charged at him again. This time around Darien barely ducked him. Fulad grazed his shield, so powerful that the slight touch threw Darien's balance off. He almost fell but was swift enough to face Fulad again.

Fulad hesitated for a moment, and dropped his sword. He had never missed and now even more rabid, he wanted to trample Darien and crush his bones with his bare burnished hands. He bolted but this time Darien decided to dart right back. With a raucous rumble stemming from his large strides, Fulad let out an even louder growl and extended his arms high enough to eclipse the sun. Running full tilt towards Fulad, Darien skidded right between his legs like a baseball player stealing a base. His legs stretched in front of him as he turned his torso, gathering enough momentum to swing his sword right across Fulad's chest.

The Zulfiqar cut through his steel skin like fire on candle wax. Darien rushed to his feet, breathing heavily. Fulad's colossal frame was also moving up and down with every breath. He reached his hand to his ribs and looked at his palm, red with his own blood. Blood he had never seen.

He started grinding his teeth uncontrollably, his eyes raging. "I'm going to make you drown in your own blood!" yelled Fulad, fists flying as he swerved towards Darien.

Darien dug his toes into the mixture of soft sand and grass below him. With a single leap Fulad was right in front of him, but Darien remained agile and cut Fulad once again on his hip. He lifted his sword over his head, stretching every muscle in his shoulders to gather enough force for his next lethal blow. But with his arms overextended and his shield by his side, he failed to see the swooping black orb until it had slammed right into his shoulder. If it wasn't for his overstretched arm, the black orb would have hit him in the face. The orb burst into violet smoke, throwing Darien to the ground. His ears began to drum louder than a military parade. His skin started to heat up as the smoke started to eat into his clothes. He immediately dropped his shield and started fanning the smoke with the sleeve of his shirt.

Fulad on the other hand was slow to turn around. His leg had given out on him. Darien's second swing had cut Fulad's hip so deep he could no longer walk. Darien, still on his back, looked up to see where the aerial object had flown in from. It was Cazi, hovering above them in front of the turret's window.

"You little swine, you hurt my only son? I am going to make your skin burn right through your flesh," she yelled in rage, causing faraway birds to scatter. It was clear now to Darien where Fulad's fury came from.

She was not a beautiful sorceress as Kafka had told him on their walk, but rather a fleeting and old woman whose pupils, black as night, veiled her sclera. The long hair floating around her was white as snow, revealed how long she must have been alive.

"Now die!" she yelled.

One orb after another appeared out of thin air as she began throwing more black spheres down on Darien. He held his shield in front of him, its Rumla coating vaporizing the violet corrosive smoke like magical sand as the orbs burst upon it.

Whilst Darien was busy covering himself, Fulad limped closer and grabbed Darien by the feet. He lifted him up and threw him into the air like a graduation cap. As Darien fell down hard, his head began to spin like a mad dervish. Cazi let out a menacing laugh as her son, drenched in blood, stood over the Golden Circle's savoir.

Φ

The melee out in the field had given Kafka an opening. Now at the top of the turret, he could hear the noises of battle coming in through the window. He stayed close to the wall, peeking out to see what was going on.

He saw Cazi floating on air and knew this was his one chance to free Evren.

"Kafka," a calm voice crept up from behind.

It was Evren. Kafka was so relieved to see him still alive that he threw his hands around the old man's neck and squeezed hard.

"I'm glad to see you Kafka too, but you need to quickly open these," said Evren, pointing at the cuffs around hands which were chained to the floor. "Darien is in trouble," Evren continued.

Kafka looked around, but the place was entirely empty. There was nothing to jimmy through the lock on the chains. He started to palpitate.

"It's ok, Kafka. It's ok. Remain calm." Evren said, seeing Kafka unnerved. "Forget about me, step out, Darien is in danger, you need to help him."

Abiding by the old man's request, Kafka stepped out of the turret's window and onto the ledge. There he saw Fulad standing over Darien and Cazi floating right above them.

"Oh no! Darien!" yelled out Kafka.

Darien looked up.

Stupid goat! He thought to himself. He had a death wish but Darien was not going to let that happen. Kafka's screech had caught Cazi's attention. She turned around and was bracing herself to throw a series of magical orbs at him when Darien in a moment of self-sacrifice aimed his shield at Cazi and threw it with all his might at her. It hit her straight in the back, scattering Rumla like fireworks into the air. The sheer power of the throw was strong enough to tilt Cazi forward. As she lost her control, Kafka saw a pearl bracelet with a key dangling from her wrist. It was the key to Evren's chains. Seizing the moment, Kafka extended his hand and snatched the key right off of her wrist. He stormed back inside, but had trouble putting the key into the lock.

He was trembling with fear.

"It's ok Kafka, stay calm, we're almost there," said Evren.

"I can't. I can't stop shaking," said Kafka whilst trying to fit the key in.

"It will all be fine in the end," said Evren. "Look at me. Look at me, Kafka. It will all be fine in the end."

Kafka could never understand how Evren always remained calm, but when he looked up and saw the old man's peaceful smile and soothing eyes, he too grew calm. He took a deep breath, forced the key into the lock, and released Evren.

Φ

Back on the ground, Darien was now defenseless. His selfless act had left him vulnerable. With no shield, he was an open mark for both Fulad and Cazi. Fulad seized the opportunity, lifting Darien and wrapping him in a bear hug.

"I'm going to make your eyes pop out of your skull," he susurrated while squeezing into Darien's chest and spine.

Darien let out a loud cry. He was in agony. He had never endured physical pain like this before and was beginning to feel life leaving his body as Fulad squeezed harder and harder. With his hands locked under Fulad's grip, the only thing he could do was flinch in pain and look down at his sword on the ground. Cazi's maniacal laughter echoed across the open plain. She was so consumed by Darien's undoing that she paid no attention to Kafka and her missing bracelet.

Darien was on the brink of blacking out when, in one bright spectacular moment, a miracle happened. The work of fate is a mystery. As Fulad squeezed, the vials on Darien's chest that were filled with Rumla began to burst and mushroom into the air. They blinded Fulad as his eyes were the only part of his body not coated in steel. The Rumla began to burn Darien's right eye as well. But not the left eye, the same one he had the parasite known as Toxoplasma dormant in. The Rumla to the parasite was like water to the desert: it consumed it quicker than a lightning strike. Darien could see through his left eye.

Fulad dropped Darien and started to rub his burning eyes furiously. Before Cazi had the chance to react, Darien sprung to his feet like a cat and ran towards his sword. He grabbed it and in one swift motion cut Fulad right through his chest cavity.

"My son!" Cazi wailed as Fulad dropped to the ground. She watched frozen as molten steel and blood flowed out of the body of her only child. Not only had her redemption turned into a cruel mirage, but she had the misery of watching as her only son died right before her black and dreary eyes. She let out a scream so loud that its sheer force lifted the rocks and leaves scattered all over the plain. Hearing the suffering in Cazi's voice, Darien felt fear for the first time on the island. Take a child away from a mother and she will bring the world to its knees for justice to be served. This much he knew from his own mother.

Cazi charged Darien, but a shadow jumped right out of the window onto the floating Cazi's back. It was Evren with Darien's shield in hand. They scuffled in midair, old foes engaged in a new clash. Cazi tried to release her hands so she could bind a spell but Evren proved too strong. They hit the sand. With no hesitation, Evren brought the shield high over his head and jammed the side of it right into Cazi's heart.

Her loud cry went deaf and she turned as still as the trees surrounding them. Her blood streamed down not far from where her son's body remained still. She was on her way to join him.

Evren knew this crime would not go unpunished.

Chapter 19
The Zomorod Box

Kafka came dashing down the stairs only to see the remains of the bloodshed. The souls of Cazi and Fulad Zereh had exited their bodies, leaving nothing but two corpses. Darien stood and watched as Cazi and Fulad's bodies deteriorated to mud in just a few seconds. The island bore an unspoken code which Darien had just discovered: when an Ashkhasi passes away, their bodies quickly disintegrate to the same material they were made out of.

The words of Papa Garibaldi echoed in the back of his mind, *the moment you are born is the moment you start dying.* He realized that death was transcendental. And no space or time could ever prevent it from happening. Even the Ashkhasis who defied the laws of time and longevity by human standards, a moment came when their life would end as well. He walked towards Evren holding the sword that dripped with Fulad's blood.

"Are you alright, Evren?" he said.

"Yes, young Darien. I am." Evren slowly got back up on his feet. There was no way Darien could tell from

Evren's emotionless face that the old man was feeling troubled inside. The murder of Cazi at his hands would have a serious consequence.

Darien's head was spinning in a rapture of bliss. The execution of Fulad and Cazi made him feel justice had been upheld in the courts of morality.

With so many hearts both on the island and in his world suffering from havoc and desolation, it was only through the strength of a sword that a new charter for piety would be ushered in.

Sensing Darien's euphoric victory worried Evren even more. There is no joy or calls for a celebration when a life is taken, even that of an enemy's. And it concerned Evren to see Darien demonstrate a trait which in the moral eyes of the universe is unacceptable. He remained quiet, as he knew words will only reaffirm what he knows Darien was feeling standing in a puddle of mud, blood and molten steel.

Evren though was not God.

His perception of Darien could not have been further from the truth. It was his own guilt of killing Cazi that wrapped around his better judgment. Darien was not embracing feelings of vengeance. He was only glad that he had given his loved ones and the entire world a fighting chance against Hubal. Darien was discovering the meaning of the empty void he had felt as a kid. In searching for himself, he had come to understand that he was defined by selflessness. This is what his purpose had been all those years he struggled to break out of conventional boundaries and a life dictated by society. A society that wanted him—

needed him—to care about money, cars, women and all the other worldly belongings. He now knew that his soul, rooted in altruism, wanted nothing more than to be a vessel to serve those in need. This was the genesis of Darien Shams, a man who had achieved self-actualization.

"Just like that? They're gone," said Kafka. "For centuries we have battled Cazi and Fulad, and, with a flick of a sword and a jab of a shield, it is suddenly all over."

Darien saw no room for words as he glared over at Tavara Hill. They had saved Evren, but now a more important matter waited. He needed to get the Ayna from the Zomorod Box and call on Alicanto as ordained by Evren. Hubal was preparing his invasion, and Darien would need to take away the life force stemming from his golden hand before he crossed the water.

"Kafka, Evren, maybe it would be best if you guys went and joined the rest," he said. He was taking charge and leading his allies, Evren included.

"You must be kidding. I've waited for as long as the sun has been around to see what's inside that box!" said Kafka as he tilted his neck forward.

Darien looked at Evren like a concerned grandson. "Evren?"

"The way you handled that sword, I think we're safer with you," replied Evren. He handed the shield back to its intended owner.

They then proceeded to move towards a wooden gazebo standing atop a tiny hill, the bodies behind them now completely crumbled.

"Evren, they just vanished into thin air," Darien said

in bewilderment.

"Yes, they did," replied Evren. His voice chirped like a bird with a broken wing.

"And the cemetery? Kafka told me it was for the deceased?"

"And he did not lie," replied Evren.

"He told me that there were others before me. How many were there?"

"This is why I admire Kafka. He says a lot. But he also knows when to remain silent," said Evren. "The tombstones you saw aren't for Ashkhasis, young Darien. Those are people from the other side of the water. Just like yourself as Kafka has already told you."

"What do you mean? I'm not sure I follow. You mean others who came before me have been buried here?" asked Darien, now more puzzled than ever.

"The plight man takes against evil is not something new. Did you think this was the first time humans have had to stand for what is right?" said Evren.

Darien had paid attention in class, and couldn't recall any stories in history or religion ever talking about fabled creatures coming into the world and conquering it. He certainly had never seen old men with facial organs on the palm of their hands.

"I know this is strange, but Hubal has not been the first to want to move across and shed a new light on humans. And he will not be the last," said Evren.

"A new light? Surely you mean cast a new darkness?" a baffled Darien replied.

Evren smiled and said, "No, shed a new light. Just

like the sun. The sun from far gives life. But get close to it and it burns anything down to ashes."

Darien felt his right hand tingle. The old man was right he thought to himself. This majestic star, so magnificent yet it could burn every cellular organism if it chose to. It could be as ruthless as it could be benevolent.

"Syoshant comes to those that are the chosen ones. We have been here before, but nobody has defeated Hubal. He is stronger and more dangerous than his predecessors, and has waited for hundreds of years to cross only when he knew his success was absolutely certain."

Evren held his stare on Darien in an attempt to try and get a read on what was going through the young man's mind.

"There's one more thing I should tell you." Evren paused right in his footsteps. "You were called to fulfill what your great-grandfather could not."

"What?" a baffled Darien interjected.

"Your great-grandfather. He never left. He was chosen, but failed to defeat Hubal," said Evren.

Darien was instantly gripped by a somber melody. His mind raced to the top of Mount Sabalan where his ancestors came from. He wished right then and there he could see his late grandfather again and tell him that his father had not truly left him. That Amir ibn Ali had a higher calling and never wished to leave his family alone to themselves. Darien had always thought it was a curse cast on the men of Shams, his grandfather having been left to build a life for his family without a father, and then

Darien's father having done the same thing to him. Hearing Evren, he wished he could hold his grandfather's hand once more and tell him that his father never deserted him. He turned from the gazebo and looked down at the mud made up of deceased bodies. He remembered his own father and how corrupt and shameless he was. Whenever anything reminded him of his father, flames would engulf his very spine and heart. Evren and Kafka both could see in Darien's big eyes the imbalance that lay in his heart. He could go in one moment from being as calm as water to as hostile as fire.

"And you tell me this now," said Darien as he squinted towards the hill in front of them.

"There is never a right time to share news that unseals gloom," replied Evren. "You see now? There is more to your story. Your dreams as a child, your frustration with people's belligerent ways and the spilling of ancestral blood are why you are standing here right now. Like I told you, you are the son of the moment."

Darien had never even seen photos of his great-grandfather but he felt his ancestor renewing his resolve. He started to move forward without waiting for Evren and Kafka, who followed behind. He reached the gazebo, bearing a simple design with cuneiform scriptures engraved all over it. Darien set his eyes only on the object that mattered now, the Zomorod Box sitting gently in front of him.

"Wait, Darien," said Evren as he grabbed him by the wrist. "This very moment, the fate of the world flows through you. Open this box with an open mind and an open heart, for it is you who will decide which way the force will swing."

Darien's eyebrows remained narrowed. He nodded his head, reached for the box, and opened it.

"What? It's not here," said Darien as he locked his jaw and drew his teeth in.

"That can't be," said Evren.

"Oh boy, are we screwed now!" echoed Kafka as he shuffled his legs back and forth like he was stuck in an invisible box.

"Wait, there's something in here." Darien saw a scroll the size of a pen rolled in the corner of the box. He looked at Evren, but the old man's face remained placid. So Darien carefully opened the scroll. This was not what he was expecting.

"What does it say?" said Evren, ever so calmly. Darien carefully recited the scroll's writings in his mind. He then took a deep breath and read what was written:

> *You open this box, looking for the celestial mirror*
> *Only to find, that empty it has been sitting here*
> *You, citizen of the universe, must learn first a lesson*
> *That a mirror is used for nothing more than to see your own reflection*
> *If Alicanto you wish to call on as a weapon*
> *Then you have to remember the origin of your essence*
> *The inscriptions were revealed to you in the Quran, Bible &*
> *Torah*
> *For you to avoid a destruction similar to the one in Sodom &*
> *Gomorrah*

*Only when your heart, your world and your faith are aligned
Will with a drop of blood, Alicanto come to save humankind*

"I don't understand?" said Kafka.

Evren was just as baffled. The apocalypse was upon them as the enigma cast on Tavara Hill unfolded.

Darien stayed mum. He could not think of anything to say. This was supposed to be Darien's destiny. Without the mirror and without Alicanto, they stood no chance against Hubal and his army. The sword and shield he carried were beginning to feel heavy. The stench of defeat was fused with the rising smell of mud.

"There is nothing for us here. We will have to go back to the Circle," said Evren as he rubbed the palm of his hands on his now gritty white robe.

"We can't just go back. We need the Ayna," said Kafka.

Darien still remained quiet as he rubbed his sleeve's soft texture on the few spats of blood on his face and forehead.

Evren for the first time did not know what to say either. It was believed that the Ayna lay in the Zomorod box which was guarded by Cazi. Those that came before Darien and succeeded never had to deal with Hubal so there never was the need to call on Alicanto, the majestic guardian of the skies. And since Hubal's arrival, no one had succeeded in defeating him including Darien's own great grandfather.

"I cannot think of where else it could be," a now worried Evren said.

Darien came from a different world and knew how manipulative God's creations could be. He looked down and saw the wind coming from beneath and lifting the leaves off the ground. "Hubal himself must have it. He knows it's his only weakness. This whole thing could be a distraction," said Darien with his voice as mellow as the wind beneath him.

Kafka nodded his head, in seeming agreement with Darien's prediction.

"No, that would not be possible. He cannot even get close to it, let alone touch it. That's why he let Cazi and Fulad watch over it," replied Evren.

Darien fixed his eyes on the wind and every miserable moment he had experienced both prior to his arrival on the island and on it flashed by in an instant. He bobbed his head but could not shake what had transpired. Then he saw himself standing with his shoulders pulling his weight down, his chin tucked into his chest hiding his eyes under his crown. He was looking at a lost soul. Yet there he stood.

Still breathing.

Darien's eyes began to tear. He remembered his playful childhood. He saw his mother standing behind them as she ran from one side of the hill to the other holding nothing more than a jug of water. He remembered how he would jump around his mother like a lion cub when she would try and find quiet moments to take a break on her bed. He remembered the teardrops that ran down the side of her face whenever she rested. Concerned, he would always say, "*Maman*, why are you crying? Please don't cry." Her response to her spirited boy was that she wasn't crying, that it was just how her eyes were. It wasn't until he got older that he realized she had only lied to her five-year-old because she never wanted him to shoulder the pain she bore being married to his father, a cad coward who had ruined their lives.

Darien looked closer and saw his sister, as she was when she was twelve, standing behind his mother with the jug and waving at him. He started to feel the agony he and his sister had felt when they were held hostage by their own father in Moscow, the frightening memories of even using the subway, where people haunted him who had been murdered for nothing more than five dollars. Two Iranian kids who hardly spoke the language had to fend for themselves, and his sister was the only beacon of strength he had during those tumultuous years.

Returning to the present, he knew he had to keep them safe. He had to prevent Hubal's nightmare from spanning all over the world. His blood boiled as he in an instant shifted back into his own refection. He lifted his head and said, "We have no choice. We must go back and we will figure it out once we are with the rest."

Kafka and Evren were less enthusiastic. They believed in the order of fate more than life itself. And if it were not meant to be, then God wanted it so.

Darien had a different interpretation of fate and very soon, it would become clear who was right.

And who was wrong.

Chapter 20
Hubal & The 360 Army

Kayret reached the murky terrain of the Tomb quicker than a ray of sun hits the earth. Having been in no rush to get to Cazi, and thinking that Darien had probably been crucified and Evren most likely burnt to ashes, he had felt no need to get Hubal's instructions to Cazi. Yet how costly that perceived luck had turned out to be. He rushed inside to the top floor where he had first carried news of Darien's arrival, but Hubal was not there. Kayret's long-limbed body quivered vehemently, shaking from side to side as though it had no spine. He ran back down and headed out of the temple, leaving a trail of dead skin all over the place. Hubal's quest must have begun. The hundred and fourteen candles upstairs in his room had been turned off. He was to eradicate the Ashkhasis of the Golden Circle and move his crusade over to the domain where humans lived.

He stormed out behind the Tomb where Hubal and his army were gearing up for their invasion. There Hubal stood behind a table with his glorious army perfectly lined up behind him. They were as still as the table in front of Hubal, the pulsating veins on their arms, necks and legs the only visible movement. Their concave armor, made of out cold gold, bounced and scattered rays of light all around.

"Your Majesty," said Kayret as he got down on one knee beside the table. He could not get himself to look at Hubal for fear of the lord with the auriferous hand losing his temper.

Hubal paid no attention. He was picking up little golden plates of armor off the table to place on the burnished chainmail vest over his arms and legs.

Hearing no response from Hubal, Kayret glanced up. The first thing that caught his eye was Hubal's curved sabre, studded with a row of spikes along its edge, and the helmet on the table. Hubal's helmet was coated in black with two massive golden horns pointing towards the sun. Kayret had sneakily once put it on. He had always wanted to know how it felt to be king. If Hubal had ever found out, Kayret would not be breathing at this moment.

"Your Majesty, I…" he begun.

"Where are the old hag and her son?" Hubal interrupted.

Kayret dropped his head to gaze at Hubal's sandals, cross tied all the way up to his knees. He began to gurgle and tremble so hard he molted right out of his skin.

"You little pest, did you not hear me?" said Hubal as he reached for his sabre and pointed it right over Kayret's head. "Did you know the boy managed to get away while you were gone?"

"Yes, yes your excellency. I-I-I…" Kayret trembled in fear.

"We are no longer going to wait. We plan to move now," Hubal continued. "Now all of the Ashkhasis are helpless without the old man. I saw weakness in that boy's eyes, and so we will wash over them like water over the shore." He paused. "Where are Cazi and Fulad with my treasure?" referring to the Ayna in the Zomorod Box.

Kayret glanced up and saw destruction in Hubal's eyes. He immediately dropped his head again and said, "I came to inform you about something I saw at Tavara Hill."

"Go on," Hubal replied as he planted his arms on the table and leaned forward.

"I know the boy got away because I saw him at Tavara Hill, your holiness," said Kayret, shuddering with every word.

"I saw him with the goat and I overheard them. They were there to set Evren free."

Hubal tried to keep his composure, smiling but tapping his fingers on the table like a marching centipede. He put his sword down and let out a gnarling growl. Raising his golden hand over his head in a clenched fist, small specks of gold and black dust started to appear out of thin air and spin around his hand. He swung his hand towards Kayret, throwing him backwards. The black and yellow fragments that had flown from Hubal's hand froze Kayret still on his back. Hubal walked around his table to stand right over him.

"I am not going to grant you death," he said as he leaned closer to Kayret's frozen face. "I'm going to let you rot here and have Dhubs come and eat into your flesh bit by bit, you pathetic little rodent." Hubal turned his peering eyes towards the Yanissaries. "The quickest pest on our island, yet also the dumbest. Now his foolishness has cost him his life."

His soldiers rustled along the incoming breeze. They could speak no words except the name Hubal. Wielding large metallic maces and swords across the island, their task would be to recite Hubal's name and make everyone remember it. They would etch his name with fear, control and force.

"The time is now," said Hubal as he went back to the table and grabbed his helmet. "I can feel victory. We have been waiting for this moment for eternity. We will march right through the Ashkhasis and take our rightful place in the so-called Creator's green pastures. We will prove to Him how weak his creations are and rule the world until the end of time."

"Hubal, Hubal, Hubal," murmured his soldiers.

"The best God and his humanity could do was send a weak little boy to stop me. I will see to his end before we march on. And the world will kneel before me and worship me as they had before worshiped God."

Φ

Little did Kayret know, Hubal was trying to hide from his formidable army any doubt that might be clouding his mind. No one before Darien had gotten this far. Hubal knew that the box was empty because it was he who had told Cazi to keep it there. He had done it to mystify the messiahs who had been summoned to come and defeat him. Truth was, he himself had no idea where the Ayna was. Alicanto had never been seen by anyone except Evren's predecessor, whom Hubal had destroyed very early on. He had spent centuries looking for it and failed to find it, but was comforted in knowing that he had overturned every rock, every tree and every corner of the island searching for it. And if he could not find it, then the Ashkhasis and the boy certainly wouldn't either.

And knowing morale in the world had reached as low as the center of the earth, this was the perfect time for him to move across the water. If he were to move swift enough then he could kill the boy, remove any possibility of anyone calling on Alicanto, and retract the prophecy. He did not need Cazi or Fulad to accomplish this. So long as his golden hand remained intact, no force, not even the sword of Zulfiqar, could hurt him. Fulad had a chink in his steel-coated skin, but Hubal's weapon was as unbreakable as his dark soul.

He proceeded to strut slowly towards his soldiers and said, "Today, we ride until the night consumes the world and we will have enslaved every man and woman by the rise of the sun."

His golden hand rumbled like nuclear fission. Digging it deep in the sand sent a tremor across the ground, breaking the surrounding trees like falling dominoes. A stampede of Sarsaoks appeared out of the dark backwoods. The Yanissaries each targeted a Sarsaok, grabbed a handful of the hair on its back, and mounted it. But the largest roared louder than the rest of behemoths. It was Tufan, a massive hare with a coat as white as porcelain. She pushed the mounted Sarsaoks to the side as she came storming towards Hubal and halted fuming right in front of him. Her eyes were bloody red as she growled. Her panting was stronger than the current of the ocean.

Hubal grabbed a golden plate and fixed it on her immaculate horn, which matched those on his helmet. "My beautiful Tufan. Make me proud today," he said as he gently brushed the fur on her cheeks.

She laid her head like a newborn foal on his shoulders as he saddled himself on her back.

"Today!" Hubal yelled as he looked across his army. "We will show Him their true nature. If His creation is immoral then so is He. And by this time tomorrow, we will have proven to God that man and his world are corrupt."

Hubal lifted his sword and pointed it to the shores on the other side of the island.

The same place where Darien had washed up unconscious only days before on the island.

Chapter 21
The Preparation

The walk back to the Circle was as silent as an oasis in the heart of the desert. The heavy hearts of the travelers captured the cadence of a winter breeze whispering over dunes. How would they share the unraveling of their saga with the rest of the Ashkhasis? There was no Ayna to call on Alicanto, and without the protector of the skies, they stood no chance of defeating Hubal.

Their demise was inevitable.

"What are we going to tell the rest?" said Kafka echoing Evren's concern as they got close to the Circle.

"The truth. We only have the truth," Evren desolately replied. He could not read Darien. He did not know whether Darien was fully aware of what was about to take place. The world that he knew was going to end. What the Ashkhasis had painstakingly avoided for so long was soon going to materialize. Humanity was not going to survive and God's creation was to be ravaged by the golden grip of Hubal. The forests across the world would scorch like one big bonfire visible to the peeping moon and stars. The dunes will be flooded with water turning into the bottom of oceans with no Arks on sight to save the animal kingdom. The world will be left to rot until the end of time arrives.

Darien had much time to think about what had just unraveled on the Hill. His expedition on Ashkhas Island had revealed to him the power of silence. In its peace and stillness he could hear his own thoughts. It was in tranquility that he could see himself. He had grown numb to disappointments and failures. His life up until that point had tested him and, although there were moments in passing that he was more than repulsed by people's actions and behaviors, he knew there was more good than bad. Failure was not an option and his words hid under his tongue for he knew better than to speak of what was prevalently obvious and certain.

They reached the Rumla floating over the meadow where the rest of the Ashkhasis stood. Darien took a glance at Evren and saw little drops of water dripping from his tightly clinched fist, tears hidden from everybody else. Darien grimaced with pain as he closed his eyes shut, and as they reached the Golden Circle, he realized that leadership was not an act of bravery but rather forbearance and the strength to move forward with humility in the belief of what is righteous. His path to justice had created a bond with these creatures. Outside his mother and sister, he had never had such a powerful affinity to anyone else. There must be more individuals like him, he thought to himself. There must be people in this world who strive to overpower what is wrong and evil and who allow their generosity and commitment to a higher cause be their moral compass. He could not let Hubal succeed. "I don't know, Evren. I don't know. Maybe if there ever was a time to lie, this might be it. I don't know how the rest will take the news," Kafka spurted out when he saw the onlookers inside the Circle notice them.

"Then how different would we be from Hubal or the people we have been sent to protect?" replied Evren.

His words surprised Darien. To this point, he had never heard anything even remotely negative from Evren, especially towards humans. But he knew better than to defend or jump at him. Something was clearly eating Evren from within. Was it the loss of the world? Was it the disappointment? Was it failure? Darien could just not tell. Perhaps when facing death, even celestial beings like the Ashkhasi could lose faith.

"Thank God. Evren you're alright!" Daena said, she and a few others rushing towards them as they entered the Circle.

"Yes, we're all fine," Evren replied.

The masses began to gather as Evren proceeded to walk towards the center of the Circle. Quiet chants and whispers were heard against the backdrop of the wind breezing harder. As the sun began to set, Evren reached the middle with Kafka and Darien beside him. All of the Askhasis surrounded them. They were delighted to see Evren safe, but Zamboor and Marmoolak had already shared the news about Hubal's preparation to invade. They waited to see what Evren would say.

Evren opened his left palm and let his words pour out. "We did not find the Ayna."

A despairing roar broke out from the crowd. Puzzled faces looked at each other and then at the news bearers. "What do you mean? Why not?" a voice rose from the crowd.

"It was not in the Zomorod box. It was not on Tavara Hill," replied Evren as he dropped his head.

The Ashkhasis waited to hear what the old man they had so relied on would say their next plan of action would be. But he said nothing else.

"So what do we do, Evren?" another voice rose.

"I don't know! Must I always say what we should do?" an enraged Evren responded.

Another wave of awe and astonishment surged from the crowd. They were all stunned, eyes wide open. As Darien looked around, their eyes reminded him of the dreadful stares he had got from his peers when he exited Baraka Capital. It was possible that none of them had ever heard Evren lose his temper for centuries. Even Kafka took a few steps back in astonishment.

But Darien did not react.

Hope had seemed to evaporate with Evren's calmness, but Darien remained calm, his feet dug sturdy into the sand like the roots of a palm tree. He was surrounded by creatures on an island that could have been an illusory figment of the imagination, but he realized that the only illusion was the very dwindling of hope. The old man had reached the zenith of hope only to not attain what he had for centuries thought was their ordained destiny. Darien needed to shift the disparaging and fading momentum. His words had until this moment remained wrapped under his tongue. Just as when somebody realizes the truth, the world has to be ready for it. And right now, they were ready.

Darien laid his hand on Evren's shoulder. A disgruntled Evren looked up at him and just as the time comes when a grandchild has to hold his grandparents hands, Darien looked right into Evren's eyes and whispered in his ear. "Dearest Evren. Your lips have grown tired, but your heart has not. Let me share my thoughts with everyone."

Evren nodded his head and took a few steps back to give Darien some space. Darien looked over everyone with piercing blue eyes like a hawk. His father had never been there to teach him to be a leader, so he had needed to teach himself about moral conduct before being able to open his mouth. This was the culmination of his metamorphosis from a man to a leader.

"Despair and fear are luxuries we do not have," he said. "I come from a world where I can complain of many things. My world is full of people with wrongful intentions. And I would be lying if I said I had not been led by those same taunts that have buried many in oblivion. I was brought to this island not because I am a savior," Darien paused and put his sword and shield on the ground. "But because I have seen and felt the good with which God has graced all of us. The love a mother gives to her child: I have felt that every day. The warmth and support a friend provides in time of need: I have felt that every day. The soul of a complete stranger that can light up the sky when you do a good deed for them: I have seen that every day."

He paused again only to look up at the clear blue sky.

"But I have learnt more about myself spending a few days with you than I ever will on the other side of the water. One thing I now believe with all conviction is that life, both here on the island and on the other side, is a mirror reflection of God Himself and we have to preserve and keep it safe from any threat at all times. Now, we have exhausted every option. There is no Ayna. And there is no Alicanto. But we have something much stronger: we have God on our side; we have God in our souls and by God we will bring Hubal and any other force looking to destroy our world down to the ground!" he said, yelling the words louder and louder.

"This world is worth fighting for and if it means I must give my life, like my great-grandfather did, then so be it. What good would an honorable life be if we lost hope now? Hubal cannot defeat us, and he will not, for we have hope. We have heart. We have faith and we have the world by our side."

He then reached for his sword and shield. He lifted it over his head and said, "Come with me. Let's stand side by side. Let's send Hubal back to where he came from and let's prove to our Creator that there are souls in this universe that stand for what He has created. Let us raise the golden sun over our heads and prove to God that indeed there is strength and honor in being righteous."

Darien's words raised a ruckus across the crowd. The Ashkhasi inhabitants thundered in hordes with some clapping hands, others stomping the ground, and all yelling out from the top of their lungs. Darien had understood by now that they were not afraid of dying for the right cause. They just needed a voice to remind them why they had been created and to inspire them to follow their golden sun.

He looked over at Evren and saw the old man's moment of weakness had vanished. Evren was overjoyed to see Darien grow into the role bestowed upon him. He leaned forward to share a few words with Darien.

"Even if we fail today when we face Hubal and his army, I will know that there is hope. Thank you, thank you for giving me the honor to show what we have stood for will not completely go in vain, for one well is enough to keep a tribe alive, and your soul is deep enough to quench the thirst of many. Remember today, Darien. Remember it well, for if we get through this, you must take this river flowing within you to those that are thirsty."

Darien smiled. There was no need for him to reply to Evren for he knew what he was talking about. He looked at Kafka and said, "So are you my ready friend?"

Kafka was even more galvanized than the rest. He had been at Darien's side through the chronicles that had brought them to this juncture. "I told you before, and I'll say it again: I'm with you till the end," he replied.

They shook hands, nodding their heads in the knowledge that their friendship had developed a soul of its own.

"And I have news for you," Darien addressed the energized Ashkhasis. "We do have a secret weapon, and that is Kafka!"

Kafka did not know where Darien was going with

this.

"Hubal has yet to feel the wrath of a Kafka ram," he said as he laughed as loud as the crowd roared.

They responded by breaking into laughter and hysterics.

"I'm sorry Kafka, I just had to!" said Darien as he shrugged his shoulders at Kafka.

Kafka just covered his eyes and swung his head side to side. With the end drawing near, no matter how it ended, they would cherish this moment. It would mark the day when a hundred and fifteen virtuous bodies stood against malevolence.

Evren felt revitalized from Darien's address as well. The verve of youth is contagious. And he was beginning to believe that they might have a chance after all. With the wisdom they have of old age, and the energy they have of the youth, they just might be able to topple Hubal's vile plan.

"We will hold our ground and we will stand behind Darien. He has yet to see how we carry the spirit of warriors under our pacifying demeanor," said Evren as he raised his fist into the air.

"Yes," Marmoolak yelled. "For it is when calm clouds gather that thunder is made!"

"Yes," Koshti howled. "We will die for those that wish to live!"

"Yes," Zamboor buzzed. "We will take the war to them if they do not want to give us peace!"

With the night on full display, the roars reverberated across the field.

"Koshti?" Evren cued the warrior.

Koshti nodded his head and stomped his foot on a nearby bed of soft leaves. The floor dropped like quicksand, revealing a slew of weapons consisting of spears, bows, arrows and curved swords with shields. Darien then understood that they were not as helpless as he had first thought. The crowd formed three straight lines and approached Koshti three at a time as he handed each one a set of weapons. Moving in an organized fashion, they then started to align right next to another like the strands in a DNA helix. The wind whistled along with the tepid shuffling of feet, paws and hooves across the field surrounded with golden Rumla.

Evren, now armed, raised his spear in the air and screamed, "Today we stand our ground and we fight. We fight for Darien. We fight for people. We fight for ourselves. And we fight for the existence of good."

The cheers were so loud that Darien closed his eyes, but he was gushing with just as much adrenaline as the rest were.

"Are you ready?" Evren yelled.

A wild wave thundered all around the Circle.

"Are you ready?" he said again, receiving an even more emphatic rumble. "Then let's march forward!"

Seven of the Ashkhasis along with Koshti jumped into the air and yelled, "Ourouboros."

The ground began to quake and the Rumla surrounding them started to whirl faster than a rotor on a helicopter. A flash, brighter than the sun, sparked and in an instant they had shifted right to the seashore.

Now all that stood in between humanity and Hubal was this sea, Darien and the Askhasis of the Golden Circle.

ك

Chapter 22
The Golden Battle

The dawn of a new day had broken free over Ashkhas Island, the battle in the sky having already begun. With the sun still on her way, a motley of purple, red, orange and blue tangled up with one another, painting the sky with a striking insignia. Today marked the Moira of Darien. The life he knew beyond the waters and the livelihood of the Askhasis who had defended it were in jeopardy. Death, one way or another, would breathe life into a new order of balance today.

He stood on the silver-encrusted sand with his back to the subtle waves of the sea. He knew he had everything to lose if they were to fail. He looked across the army before him and knew they shared his sentiment. The Ashkhasis began to hum as they rattled their ivory tipped spears, wooden carved bows and brass plated swords. The hypnotizing sound of the percussion sent Darien into a rapture and with each chime his fear of failure washed further back into the open sea with the waves. The Ashkhasis maintained their rhythm as suddenly their handheld weapons lit up like torches. Their flame was as strong as the sun herself. The Ashkhasis' display of strength and courage exhilarated Darien.

"See, we're not as helpless as you may have thought," smiled Kafka while holding his lit shield and sword.

"There was never any doubt in my mind. And there is definitely none in my heart," replied Darien. He could feel the rays of the sun flowing right through his body.

As the dulcet melodies of their shields and arms ensued, a cloud of sand began to gather down the shore by the green woodlands Darien had roamed in for the past several days. As the dust began to settle, they could see Hubal and his army standing a few hundred feet away from them. Hubal pulled tight on Tufan's mane as she halted to a stop.

Hubal closed his eyes and took in a deep breath. "Ah, I can smell victory. I get aroused by this smell," he said. "The time has come for the stars to lose their way in the sky and the mountains to vanish under water. I am going to fold the sun before their very eyes. Soon, I will be God to all."

He smiled at every word he uttered. The rolling growls of the Sarsaoks along with their heavy legs thudding on the ground muted the clattering of the Ashkhasis. Hubal knew that the end had approached and Darien and the Golden Circle's denizens stood no fighting chance without Alicanto. His pride and ego dwarfed his desire for victory for he stood across them and just stared across. He wanted to bask in the moment before he and his army pummeled them to the very ground they rose from. Hubal remained still on Tufan's back. In his mind, he had already won the battle. Everything that would arise from this point on was just a matter of his holy revelation's history.

"Hold your ground everyone. We will wait for them to make the first move," said Evren as he held his spear parallel to the ground.

Darien fidgeted with the grip on his sword in his right hand. They were outnumbered, but the strength and courage in their hearts made up for the lack of bodies. He could see Hubal's luminous right hand lighting up like a lantern. He had never met his great-grandfather but he still yearned for vengeance. He would make Hubal pay for he had appointed himself both jury and judge in the name of his grandfather, who had suffered so much without the presence of a father.

Darien was void of anxiety. Standing in between the Ashkhasis and Hubal, he remained mindful. He knew the only way to kill a snake swiftly was to cut off its head. If he could take Hubal out, then the rest of his soldiers, like the remains of a headless snake, might rattle but would impose no harm. Killing Hubal would keep humanity alive and save the lives of the Ashkhasis. Then he had an idea.

"Evren," Darien whispered.

Evren faced him but before Darien could continue, Hubal's voice broke the silence from across the field. "Who wears the throne today?"

There was no response.

"I said who wears the throne today?"

Still no response, Hubal's livid voice having even silenced the Sarsaoks.

Hubal grinned in anger and slowly said again, "Who wears the throne today?"

"Those words are only reserved for the Almighty on Judgment Day," Evren spoke up as he pointed his spear in Hubal's direction. "Today, free will's emissary along with us will bring you to your knees."

A boisterous applause erupted behind him.

Hubal's eyes narrowed as he scowled. "I'll make sure you and the rest of your pathetic companions watch me as I pull your heart out of your chest, you ignorant fool!"

Darien felt the strain in Hubal's voice. Their buoyancy along with their elation infuriated Hubal. He wanted to break their hope before killing them all, and an enraged Hubal would mean a swift execution. He knew if there was any chance of defeating him, he would need Hubal to remain calm.

"Evren," said Darien. "I have a plan, but I first need to ask you a question and I need you to be sincerely honest with me." Evren turned and gave his undying attention to Darien.

"Do you believe in the prophecy? Do you believe in me?" he said.

"Of course. We all do," replied Evren.

"Then if I were to make a request, would you honor it?"

The eleventh hour had struck, and sparing a dying man's wish was something Evren could not live with—even if that may be for a short period of time. "Anything Darien."

"Then I ask you to follow my lead," said Darien as he

tilted his sword forward. "I will face Hubal. You decide what you and the rest should do after, but no matter how it ends I ask you to not march forward until you see the last breath leaving my body."

"We've come this far together, we can't just let you face him alone," replied Evren in astonishment.

"I am not facing him alone. I have the hope of you and billions resting on my shoulder. If I fail, then so be it. But you and the world should..." he paused momentarily. "You and the world *must* prevail. Hold the rest back and you can then decide what to do when you see him standing over my body."

There was no space or time for Evren to turn down Darien's sacrificial request. He nodded his head and then whispered to Koshti to tell the rest to hold their positions. He then turned to Darien and said, "Alright young Darien, you have my word."

Darien smiled to calm the adrenaline tensing his body. He looked across the field and yelled, "Hubal!"

Darien's clamor caught Tufan's attention. The big beast with the golden horn snarled and took a few steps forward. Hubal had to rein the creature back.

"You are no God. No man or woman will bow down to you. We know we are outnumbered. We know what your soldiers are capable of. But what about you? What kind of deity are you if you need help to claim your divine place?" said Darien.

Hubal did not budge, despite Darien's desperate taunts. This was not the first time he had heard a creature facing death sing to the tune of a jester's song.

"Why don't you prove your worth and face me in the middle of the field?" said Darien as he clapped his sword and shield together.

The only response he got was a loud laugh in sync with Tufan's fuming breath.

"Face me and if I fall to your sword then the rest will lay down their arms and serve you for as long as you need them to."

Darien's words sent a wave of scoffs from behind. The Askhasis had come to fight. Submission to Hubal's evil parade was not their ordained destiny. Evren motioned to keep the crowd calm and let them know that there was a plan in place.

"Yes, now I know who you are," said Hubal with a satisfied smile. "You are the son of Shams! My my, how the mighty rise, and how the mighty fall. You're Shams' offspring." Hubal paused squinting as he looked towards Darien's direction. "He bore courage like yourself. But I made quick work of him just like I will with you," he said pointing his golden hand to the young man. "Death will be the gift I bear to you in so long as when you see him again, remind him how I dug my sword right through to his heart."

Darien began to grind his teeth. He wanted to charge towards his great-grandfather's murderer.

"Then let it be known today that Hubal will sit on the throne," Hubal yelled as he turned to face his soldiers. "And your blood will dry on this island along with your ancestors and you will be nothing but a distant memory once the sun sets."

"I stand for who all love this universe. It will be you who will remain here," said Darien as he held tight on his arms.

He began to take short but quick strides on his toes towards Hubal and his army. Hubal gave the big beast he straddled a nippy kick and Tufan galloped forward. Darien began to run. He ran as if his heels had grown a pair of miraculous wings. He could feel the wind and the sand jumping up in the air with every pace he took towards his destiny. Hubal matched his every stride as they got closer to one another.

Evren looked up in the sky and then at Kafka and everybody else behind him who throughout the whole exchange had grown afraid and said, "The sun is about to rise. No matter what happens, don't lose sight of the light within you." Then darting forward he murmured under his breath, "For darkness is the absence of light."

But nobody heard what he said.

Chapter 23
The Duel

Darien bolted towards Hubal, remaining so focused on charging that he failed to see a trailing Evren behind him. Hubal, seeing Evren sprawling behind Darien, was infuriated. They had not kept their word, and in retaliation he raised his golden hand and pointed it straight towards the sky. It sucked in air from all around it and radiated piercing golden flecks and rays. Darien braced himself to dodge the skin-thawing pellets thrust out of Hubal's hand. Hubal flung his hand forward, shooting thousands of blinding little pellets of light towards Darien.

Little did Hubal know that in the midst of all the chaos on the island Darien had found peace. He had found order within disorder. As the golden tide of explosions got closer, Darien nudged his shoulder to his side and steered clear of the projectiles. Hubal heaved a series of golden slugs, one after the next. Each of them targeting the approaching Darien. Darien leaped over them as though he was reenacting the eve of the Wednesday before the Persian New Year. A ceremony known as *Charshanbeh Soori* when Persians make bonfires and jump over them asking the fire to take away pain and suffering and gift them with courage and light. Hubal lobbed one golden bullet after the next right out of thin air, but missed with every throw.

Now they were mere feet away from one another. Darien hid his shoulder behind his shield and covered his head as he braced for his collision with Tufan. Hubal tilted his head back in surprise. What sane person would charge right at a beast stronger, more agile and larger than an elephant? What he didn't know was that Darien's tactic was to slide right through the rigid springs that were Tufan's legs. Darien saw openings between every gallop Tufan took and planned to use the same ploy he did in defeating Fulad.

Hubal wasn't going to let his moment be ruined by having his steed trounce all over the world's savior, so he jumped right off Tufan and ran towards Darien. With his head covered by his shield, Darien could not see Hubal raise his foot before ramming it right into him, sending Darien flying backwards.

Darien quickly got to his feet. He had Hubal where he wanted. He rushed towards him, wielding his blade back and forth like a hummingbird's wings. But Hubal dodged each of Darien's violent swings by bobbing his body and head like a seasoned boxer. Then he grabbed Darien by the wrist.

"You can slay goats. You can cut through steel with this blade," said Hubal. "But you will need a lot more than that to get through me." Hubal squeezed Darien's arm and tossed him to the ground like a hand full of mud.

Darien was running short on breath. He got back up and grabbed his sword as Hubal just stood there, toying and taunting Darien. Hubal wanted to break Darien before the Ashkhasis and send a message to God that he was just as powerful. Darien this time swung his shield to distract Hubal, jabbing his sword with the other hand. His attempt was futile; Hubal grabbed his shield like it was a coin and lifted him, still strapped to his arm, up in the air. The sun's rays pierced Darien's eyes as he let out a groan.

"I'm going to break your soul before I break your bones," said Hubal as his lips curled revealing golden teeth. He pitched his hand backwards and slammed it into Darien's shield with all his might. It shattered it into a million pieces, knocking Darien down once more to the white sand.

Darien was running on fumes. He had no more energy to get back up on his feet. He rolled to his side and saw Evren on his back, chest open, lying still and breathing heavy. The first golden bolt Hubal hoisted had hit Evren. He had broken Darien's promise only to try and keep him safe.

"No. No, Evren," Darien whispered as he raised his hand, fingers extending as far as they could towards where Evren lay in gold dust and blood.

Hubal this time did not give Darien the chance to get back up on his feet. "You are the one?" he growled as he wrapped his hand around Darien's neck. "You are the one God sent?"

Hubal lifted him off the ground. Darien began to choke as Hubal dug his sharp ochroid nails into Darien's throat. Life began to leave his body as he tried to grasp for air. Hubal clenched a handful of Darien's long hair with his other hand and tugged his head back.

"Look at you! You couldn't even save the old man," said Hubal as he snapped Darien's neck back, sending a thousand thorns pulsing down Darien's spine and his dangling legs.

Darien grabbed onto the hand with which Hubal had shrouded his jugular. He looked down and saw the shattered pieces of his shield that bore the sun's reflection like a broken mirror. This was a bad omen. The old adage where a broken mirror brings bad luck must be true.

"Before I take your life, I want to look into your eyes and let you know that when I am on the other side, I will take exceptionally good care of your loved ones," whispered Hubal as he gazed into Darien's gradually closing eyes. His nails were dug so deep that a strand of Darien's blood began to drip from the edge of Hubal's palm.

This was it. His great-grandfather's fate had too fallen upon him. Everything was going black. He could not feel the sun's presence any longer. In that very dark moment, he saw his mother and sister's faces. He heard his grandparent's voice. He felt the joy of the huddles he had shared on the football pitch with his friends. The smell of his first girlfriend's perfume rushed through his nostrils. He saw a collage of the endless and calm dunes of the UAE. He saw the rough yet majestic mountain ranges of Iran's Zagros Mountains. Remembrances of the boundless forests of New England and Russia through his younger years flashed right before him. Hubal's laugh echoed further and further away with every breath he struggled to take. He was passing out. The end had approached and there was only one other thing left for him to do and that was to pray.

He closed his eyes and shared his last words with God.

"Please, I beg you. I beg you to forgive whoever allows Hubal in their hearts." As he shared his last words, he looked up as he did not want the last thing his eyes recorded to be Hubal's grody face. His eyelids were giving up on him.

But then he heard a familiar voice.

"Only when your heart, your world and your faith are aligned. Will with a drop of blood, Alicanto come to save mankind." It was the voice of Syoshant. The same angel that came to his dream and brought him here.

Hearing his voice, Darien had a sudden surge of energy. He glanced around for hope of seeing Syoshant but he was nowhere on sight. Hubal hadn't flinched which made Darien think that the voice he heard was in his own head. He mustered what little energy he had left and tried to break free once more from Hubal's grip, but failed as Hubal squeezed even harder. Darien let out a loud cry.

"To hell with this! We can't just watch them die!" yelled Kafka.

Watching Evren fall and now Darien, the rest of the Ashkhasis were on edge as much as Kafka was.

"Evren, sorry for breaking your word," whispered Koshti. He raised his sword. "Let's charge! Down to every last one of us! We will send these varmints back into the abyss!"

They charged single file towards the middle of the field where Darien and Hubal were tangled up. Hubal's soldiers responded, galloping into the fray.

Darien could hear stomping and distant screams of fury as the ground trembled beneath. He had failed to keep them safe.

Hubal let out a loud laugh and said, "You'll be put out of your misery soon." A stream of Darien's blood flowed smoothly over Hubal's hand and down to his elbow as he squeezed Darien's neck tighter. It flowed smoothly on his golden hand right down to his elbow. With his hand bent, there was no other place for Darien's blood to go other than drip on to the soft sand he had his hands and legs dug deep in earlier.

The first drop hit the sand.

Only when your heart, your world and your faith are aligned. Will with a drop of blood, Alicanto come to save mankind.

As soon as Darien's blood had stained the sand red, a loud scream echoed across Ashkhas Island. It was a sound Darien had never heard before, but everybody else on the shore seemed to recognize it.

A gathering nimbus obscured the sun's light and out from the gathered clouds looped and coiled the guardian of the avian world. With a trail of inferno in her wake, it was Alicanto: Hubal's biggest fear and only worthy adversary was now swirling right over his head. His jaw dropped as he released his grip on Darien's neck. Darien fell to his knees, looking up in time to see the aerial assault reverberating across the sky. Alicanto was magnificent. The crimson red and bright yellow feathers of her wings stretched as wide as a plane. Her golden claws glittered on her long and colorful tarsi. She unhinged her strong beak and let out another scream.

"No, this cannot be!" said Hubal in awe. He was idle still. There was no Ayna and he had yet to comprehend how Alicanto appeared. Darien grabbed a handful of sand and whispered, "Only when your heart, your world and your faith are aligned. Will with a drop of blood, Alicanto come to save mankind."

This was the third constitutions of his life's covenant. It was *faith* in God and the belief that the world was indeed good. He had fulfilled the three constitutions written in the scroll with his last prayer, fulfilling his prophecy. He now understood the scroll. The answer did not lay in a box. It did not lay in some magical weapon. It was within Darien all along. He was unaware at that point that the constitutions he had reached to were unravelling on the island all along, way before he even read the scroll. And if it hadn't been for Hubal shedding his blood, Alicanto may have never come.

The royal bird swooped in, her shadow getting larger and larger on the sand. Hovering right over Hubal's soldiers, she flapped her massive wings, sending them flying through the air in all different directions. She looped back up into the air once again and, locking her sight on Hubal, rocketed from the sky towards him. Hubal panicked as he braced himself to run back into the green labyrinth, but was too late. She was already above him.

Hubal only managed a few steps before she dug her massive claws right into his golden hand, ripping it in one fluid motion. It set off a golden combustion. The wind from under her broad wings was so powerful that it almost threw Darien on his back. Alicanto soared back up in the air, turning over her shoulder and looked right at Darien. He could see right into her penetrating turquoise eyes.

On the ground, Hubal stood with an amputated arm. He looked around and saw the devastation Alicanto had caused. He was breathing heavy as blood and golden particles shot out of what remained of his hand. He paid no attention to Darien, who seized the moment to roll towards his sword a few feet away. He grabbed it and jumped towards Hubal.

"You end today," he screamed as he dug his sword deep into Hubal's chest.

Hubal's eyes widened open as he tried to gasp for air. He looked down and saw the double-edged sword protruding from his chest cavity.

Hubal looked right at Alicanto, flying circles above them, and began to laugh drolly. But the laugh came to a halt as he grabbed Darien's wrist once again and welded the sword deeper into his own chest. He pulled Darien close and laid his coarse lips on his ear.

"You think it's over? You think this ends today?" Hubal struggled to breathe, gurgling in his own blood, as he found some air for his last departing words. "This is just the beginning. As long as you live, so will I."

And before Darien could say anything, Hubal fell to his knees as his eyes rolled to the back of his head. He fell to his side, still breathing heavy. Darien stood over him and screamed out at the top of his lungs as he pounded his chest three times. His rage had got the best of him.

He cast his shadow over Hubal's corpse as it began to disintegrate—just as Cazi and Fulad's had.

Darien, the anointed one, had succeeded where his predecessors had failed. Good had finally prevailed where evil existed.

Chapter 24
The Aftermath

There were no more squawks from the sky above. With Hubal's body fading Alicanto started to fade. The mighty bird with the golden hand clutched in her claws had flown towards the star at the center of our solar system. Darien's eyes shifted towards the sun while his heart palpitated. Even now that Hubal was gone, he could not calm himself.

"It's over, Darien," said Kafka as he walked over and placed his hand on his shoulder. "It's over."

It's over. It's over. It's over. Darien kept reciting Kafka's words in his mind until it drifted off. He had managed to save humanity from enslavement, but there was a morbid feeling boiling inside that he could not identify. Was it that his adventure had come to an end? Was it that for the first time he had followed a task through to the end? Was it that the lives of Ghoul, Fulad and now Hubal hung heavy on his heart? Or was it the words Hubal had quietly gasped in his ear before Darien's sword took his life? All he knew was that the prophecy which Evren had recited had now been fulfilled.

"Evren," he jolted as he snapped out of his reverie.

He ran towards where Evren lay. A few of the Ashkhasis had gathered around him, and he was still alive, but there was not much they could do to save the voice that had served as their guide for so long. The island had rules and the price one paid for taking a life was to give their own. This was the unspoken code amongst the Golden Circle's inhabitants.

Darien kneeled down and lifted Evren's ailing head to his shoulder.

"Shams, the golden Shams," said Evren as he coughed and touched Darien's hand.

Darien embraced Evren's fatherly touch. The old man, in just a few days, had managed to fill an empty well in Darien's heart. He had grown not only fond of but attached to the old man who always wore a smile. Darien's eyes began to fill with water. The scent of the most celestial flowers flooded his nostrils; he always used to think how in such moments of sorrow people often missed the opportunity to savor the smell of melancholy.

"You are a stubborn old man, Evren" he said as a tear dropped on Evren's hand.

"I'm sorry, Darien. I'm sorry for showing weakness. We are not very different. I had lost hope, but thanks to you, I believe again," said Evren. His words were interrupted by a slow medley of coughs. "Remember what you have learnt here today. Take it with you, and share it with everybody else."

"You can't die, you can't leave!" cried out Darien, no longer able to hold his emotions back.

"I'm not leaving, young Shams," replied Evren. He paused and, for the first time, his face began to dance. Now his lips began to speak for him. "I am not leaving for I am only arriving."

And with those last whispered words, Evren's eyelids closed shut. Darien clutched Evren's hand with the eye in his palm and held it close to his forehead. He closed his eyes and held Evren's palm on his forehead until his body began to crumble bit by bit. Darien began to cry. The gravel in his gut became heavier as the body beneath his hands turned into nothing else but ash-laden sand. Kafka, standing next to him, and the surrounding Ashkhasis were in pain. They had lost one of their own and it was their hearts that ailed for they would not hear his voice again for a very long time.

"This was inevitable, Darien," said Kafka. "It is a natural law on our island. The moment Evren took Cazi's life he knew his fate was determined."

Darien looked up at Kafka, eyes still drenched. "But he died protecting me. He did that to protect us. Why the punishment?"

"Punishment?" Kafka said in bewilderment. "There is no punishment. He is with his maker now. Besides, murder is murder. Does it make it right that it was a just cause? I cannot answer that. We cannot answer that."

Darien knew Kafka had a point. He remembered how his sister always would boast about what a high moral standard Darien liked to maintain. There had been many times when people around him had broken his moral law. It started with statesmen, leaders of tribes who drove their

236

people to death by greed and power—weaknesses that percolated down to his own personal life: his philandering fiancé and his selfish and vengeful father. Darien had tasted immorality too many times close to his own heart. He always searched for moral justice, but deep down inside he knew two wrongs never added up to one right. Drenched in blood, sweat and tears, worn down by his battle with Hubal, he was at a loss for words. Victory was not supposed to taste so bitter. He knew there was nothing to say to bring Evren back except cherish his last words. He was with the One who created it all, regardless. Mourning was really for the living. More for his own loss than Evren dying. So although he mourned deep inside, Darien too celebrated knowing Evren at that very moment danced and twirled like a bedlamite in the sky. Evren now dwelled on the grandest of islands, where water and fire waltzed side by side. He had risen from the core of the earth but now was at the core of it all. He was with God.

Never had Darien ever questioned God's existence and throughout the adversity on the island, his heart, his world and his faith had aligned. Even if it was for a fleeting moment, he had the chance to take a sip from an oasis surrounded by an arid land. A taste was all it took for him to get intoxicated. There is verity in the saying that you speak the truth when drunk. Now Darien was a drunk amongst drunks. His heart danced to the most beautiful tunes dithering from the strings, repercussions and bells of heaven. He could not wait to join Evren more than even going back and kissing his mother's forehead or hugging his sister tighter than the oxygen she longed for on top of the mountains she climbed.

Darien would do his best to honor Evren's word and let his universe know that the only key to life was aligning your heart, your world and your faith—as he had kept them aligned throughout the adversities he had faced on the island. This alignment was more divine than happiness. For happiness is nothing more than an emotional euphoria. A mental state of mind with a physical combustion of chemicals in the body as a result of a human thought. What Darien felt was more than a chain reaction of mental and physiological reactions.

Darien wiped his sweat with his wrist. "So what happens now?"

"Now," said Kafka as he got down on his knees bringing his brown eyes to the same level as Darien's. "Now is time for you to go home."

Chapter 25
The Farewell

"We have to get you ready while the sun is still up," said Kafka.

Darien did not hear him as his mind drifted to the same place where silence plays the loudest melody. He remained still until Kafka tapped him several times on his shoulder. He turned and looked at him with the same serene smile Evren wore for all the centuries that flew by. He had never felt more mindful.

"Hello! You still here?" Kafka said sarcastically.

Darien smiled. He remembered his freshman year when he had been just as submerged in his own heart. He had driven from Boston to New York with his mother, who was concerned for her son when all he did was lay down in the back of their black Ford Explorer. This car, he remembers the model. He had been so quiet that she thought he was on drugs, but whenever they recalled the story now, they would always laugh. It wasn't the recreational substances that had Darien mystified. It was the realization that the closer he looked, he noticed how life's mundane moments were miracles and the real miracles were everyday's mundane moments. He had drowned in a trance of self-actualization that made him loose appetite for food, for small talk and for conforming to societies norms. He was as mindful as ever during his freshman year, even though everybody including his mother thought he was drifting in another dimension.

"I am Kafka, I am still here," Darien softly replied.

Kafka was not exceptionally comfortable with goodbyes. He sat next to Darien and drew little circles in the sand with his hooves, unable get himself to look up. "I can't believe he's gone," he finally said.

"He is where he should be. We will all join him at one point," replied Darien.

He dragged his leg over the circles Kafka drew in the sand to grab his attention. Darien's journey had transformed him, and he knew that Kafka now smiled at him for he saw that Darien had now grasped the ways of the Ashkhasis through their preference for direct eye contact.

"Yes he is, and we will miss him," said Kafka as he looked into Darien's eyes.

"They are here Kafka," said Koshti as he walked over and stood by Kafka's side.

Darien said, "Koshti, you are the most noble of warriors I have ever met. It has been an honor to spend what little time we had on this island together."

Like most warriors, Koshti expressed himself with gestures and not words. So he stuck his hand out to shake Darien's. They locked grips as the rest of the band—Marmoolak, Zamboor, Daena, Kharteet and all the rest—

gathered around.

"So what happens to you guys now?" said Darien as he looked at each of them.

"Now, we wait," replied Daena.

"Wait, for what?"

"We live as we did before until the others join us from Agartha," carried on Kafka.

Darien saw no need to get into details. Evren had to be replaced. He knew that much. Hubal had been right: as long as humans lived, so would the Ashkhasis. Darien had stepped into a beautiful world where love reigned supreme and God could be seen everywhere. He was now intoxicated, but the harsh reality was that the world he came from was far from utopia. He knew going back that there was still plenty that needed to be done and it would be only be a matter of time before another replaced the empty void Hubal left behind.

"These belong to you," interrupted Kharteet. He handed over Darien's tuxedo, dried and clean.

"Thank you. Thank you all," said Darien as he stared into everybody's face. "I will cherish every moment I spent here and it has been a privilege to have met you all."

They smiled and one by one came by to shake his hand. Kafka waited until the rest were done paying their homage to the anointed one. The gloom thick in the air proved that the Ashkhasis felt as if one of their own was departing.

"I sure as hell am going to miss you, Kafka," said Darien as he smiled at Kafka saving the best for last.

"So will I, Darien."

"Will we meet each other again dear friend?" asked Darien.

"Meet? Probably not. But see? All the time."

They did not exchange goodbyes for Darien knew the time would come when he would see his friend again.

"Abtu and Anet will guide you with Zaratan," said Kafka.

Darien looked over to the water and saw the two feisty fish jumping out of the water. "Zaratan?" he questioned.

"Zaratan is your ride back to where you drifted out here from."

"Please tell me it's a horse with wings," Darien said, knowing humor was the garment Kafka was most comfortable wearing.

Kafka laughed, relieved that Darien was taking this all well.

"It's even better! You'll see in a bit."

As they stood and waited on Zaratan, the two recollected the short memories they now shared. Kafka spoke about the first moment he saw Darien and how petrified he had been, irony of it all being that they now stood in the same place where Darien had tried to drown himself and wake from what he thought was a dream. As they joked and laughed, large bubbles like the hurling geysers of Iceland burst out of the nearby water. Darien saw a turtle's shell as large as a helipad surface from the sea. Darien pointed at it and looked at Kafka with an eyebrow up.

"Yup, that's Zaratan," said Kafka, nodding his head.

"Just one thing: when you're off the island you will no longer speak Lisan, so whatever these two troublemakers say you will not understand," he pointed at Abtu and Anet.

"When you arrive, Zaratan will stop, and that's when you have to jump back into the water. There are people searching for you on the other side and they will find you."

Kafka's words were all mere details of the larger picture Darien was seeing and feeling. "Don't worry about me. You just worry about yourself," he said as he stretched his hand out to Kafka.

Kafka sniffed the hand, slapped it away, and threw himself in for a hug. "Remember what you have learnt here. For Evren at least," he said as he held onto Darien tight.

Darien wrapped his hands around Kafka. His fur was grainy, but his heart was smooth. "I will, dear Kafka. I will carry the message."

Darien turned and swung his hand through the Rumla around the Circle for one last time. He walked into the water and jumped on Zaratan's shell. He glanced over his shoulder just as Alicanto had and Kafka stared right into Darien's eyes as they camouflaged with the color of the sea and sky.

With one step, Darien now was off the island. Kafka had forgot to share his parting words, so he ran into the water and started to yell words now sounded foreign to Darien.

Darien squinted and tilted his head sideways to hear.

"Led need aynod! Teday hehsab!" yelled out Kafka.

"What?" Darien yelled back.

"Led need aynod. Teday hehsab!" he yelled again as loud as he could.

Darien smiled and nodded his head. "I will, Kafka. I will."

◊

Chapter 26
The Zaratan Ride

The island began to shrink as Zaratan floated further and further into the deep dark waters of the sea. Darien stood from far and watched as the Rumla enveloped around the turf the Ashkhasis stood on spin and then vanish. And just like that, they were gone with nothing remaining except for an alluring Emirati island's shore.

Darien gazed across the sea's endless horizon. It was a mirror reflection of the sky above. As his eyes stared across, the sounds and motions around him began to slow down. Even Abtu and Anet's acrobatic leaps out of the water were beginning to fade in front of his very eyes. Their back and forth tête-à-tête muted with each placid wave that hit Zaratan's carapace. As he looked at Zaratan's bony shell, he noticed identical overlapping circles in a perfect geometric juxtaposition cemented on it. Zaratan's back bore the seal of the flower of life, the same insignia he had stared a thousand times on the clock hanging in his room.

Darien felt a little weight hanging in his left pocket. He dug his hand in only to feel the textures of his golden encrusted watch. He took it out and held it in front of himself. His Rolex had started to tick again. He had been holding on to the wrong things for so long. All this time, he had been chasing the wrong dream. He no longer needed either. Neither the possessions nor time itself so he hurled the watch into the water. He remembered Abu Faris' story and the day he caught a golden pearl in the same waters he was drifting on. He felt his feet clogged out of air in his designer Italian loafers. He needed them to breathe so he took his shoes out one by one and threw it in the ocean as well. He now could feel Zaratan's shell which was as crude as his idea on life had been to this point. He took two steps and stood right in the middle of Zaratan's shell. As he stood there he thought of the illusion that separated him from life and God throughout all these years. His mind was deceived and his heart was consumed by thoughts that had drifted him further from the real truth. The one absolute truth that life is nothing more than a series of events and memories and the only way to understand it is to step out of worldly desires and step into the Circle of God.

There was a blessing that was bestowed on Darien during his days on Ashkhas Island. He had shed all of his fears, his pain and his illusion on what reality meant. He was immersed in a world of fantasy where bizarre creatures spoke, yet it was more real than any moment he ever felt or experienced.

And as Zaratan glided forward, he knew he was getting closer to appearances and illusion and further away from reality.

Take this river flowing within you for those that are thirsty. Those were the last departing words of Evren. It all began to make sense to Darien. He was not special. He was not unique.

He was not the messiah.

He was everyone and every living creature in one ecstatic motion. His constant apparitions were nothing more than a gentle reminder from God that he was in sync with the world's beating heart. God had not knighted him as mankind's savior for Hubal was right. Darien was nothing more than a peasant in God's vast kingdom. He bore a message only from a small glimpse he got of God's glorious paradise.

The same nirvana marked on Monish's catamaran is where Darien resided now and his message was simple. He was to let the world know that the only wealth that mattered was affinity and generosity. Affinity towards oneself and generosity towards the world itself. The inhabitants of the world no longer needed to hide behind shiny objects. There was no more need for worshipping brands on cars, clothes and jewelries like the pagans did. There is no longer a need to hide behind photo filters.

You are most beautiful in your purest form. You are a manifestation of God himself. Open your eyes and let the light flow right through to your core. All it takes is for you to notice a flicker of leaves, a momentary glance from a loved one, or for a wave to hit your toes and freeze you in that timeless place where you know with every cell in your body that God, indeed is real.

Darien was now committed to letting go of worldly

possessions and pursuing the only wealth that mattered which would be his soul's nourishment.

He was going to embrace love every day. He would appreciate the world every hour. And he will believe in God every second. For he now knew that with those three constitutions, he will have a feeling of immense wealth that binds him to everyone, with everything in life and with every little particle that makes up the universe's Golden Ratio.

Darien could hear the mighty yet gentle words of the zephyr twirling around him. He knew his real mission was only to begin. He will need to show justice for those who seek it. He will have to bring knowledge to those who demand it. He began to look around the melodic tunes the sea, sky and the wind orchestrated. It was the sound of tranquility. It was the sound of silence.

And it took his breath away.

He thought to himself, "How many times have I been to these waters? How many times have I swum, jet-skied and sailed in these waters? Never had I noticed its pristine and magical beauty. All this time, I searched for a sign, an inspiration from God to wake me up. And it was in front of me, it was around me, it was inside of me all this time."

Zaratan reached to a sojourn. Darien knew it was his time to jump out into the water. He took in a deep breath and looked around. Abtu and Anet were no longer there. He stepped to the edge of Zaratan's shell and plunged right in. Zaratan slowly submerged into the water like a God made submarine. There was no longer a visible sign of life from the Ashkhas Island.

He paddled while noticing how quiet the water was. Yet, under its surface, a world of life and liveliness brewed that was only visible to one deep underwater. Darien smiled for he knew no one would believe his stories. He would have to cover his ecstasy just as the water does to the life brewing underneath it.

Breathe. Only breathe Darien thought, while he calmly stayed afloat the water's current.

The tides around him grew stronger. This time around, he had no regrets as he stayed afloat and let nature take its course. With every wave that came in, he began to feel lighter.

His chest began to open up as he took deep breaths in. And before he knew it, he blacked out with his tuxedo and a new state of complete consciousness.

و

Chapter 27
The Coma

Darien slowly opened his eyes. He could see faint shadows of three phantoms hovering over him, but could barely hear their voices behind the ear-deafening din of blades cutting through the air. Darien's first thought was that he was back on Ashkhas Island. The heaving emphatic vibration resembled that of the Rumla-sheathed Circle when it beamed to another spot on the island. He felt a tight pull on his chest and legs. He could not move his neck. As he started to regain his vision, he attempted to raise his head again only to be interrupted by a hand that pressed on the side of his shoulder.

"Relax, stay still, everything is alright," the voice said.

Darien regained his depth of field and saw a man in a navy blue suit and bright orange jacket look at him with a comforting smile. Next to the man was another, younger with a perfectly trimmed beard, who spoke through a transmitter sticking out of his large blue helmet. He heard this man say, "He's ok, *Alhamdulillah*. He just woke up."

The man was speaking Arabic. Darien was back home.

Another voice jumped in. "You lucky son of a gun! You're alive!" It was Samer, who had been sitting behind a few safety vests, oxygen masks and what Darien assumed were parachutes.

Darien raised his head and saw that the two men were steering a helicopter, one pressing the pedals and the other fidgeting with the dashboard buttons and cyclic. Darien now realized the roaring sound was the mechanical whirlwind of the helicopter's gyro. The first thought he had was that he had been rescued. The second thought that came rushing to Darien's mind was whether everything he had been through had just been a dream. He remained silent, staring at Samer and the two coastguards dressed in their blue attire.

"Are you alright? Is he alright?" said Samer swaying his question from pilot to pilot.

The man who still had his hand on Darien's shoulder said, "*Na'am* he is ok. He just is coming to conscious."

With what little broken Arabic Darien spoke, he understood what the man had said. "I'm fine," he said, finally breaking the silence. He still couldn't lift his body up. He lay his head back on the bed they had him lying on and heaved a loud sigh.

"Darien, are you alright?" a worried Samer again asked.

Darien, though, was elsewhere, for he could not tell whether all that he had been through had been just a lucid dream. Could it have been that Kafka, Evren, Hubal and all of the events on Ashkhas Island had been nothing more than a series of shams?

His head began to throb as reality sobered him: his time on Ashkhas Island had been as much an illusion as Syoshant. He closed his eyes hoping to drift back to his dream again.

Samer, now even more concerned for his friend, shook him until Darien opened his eyes again. "Darien, please say something!"

Darien knew he could not go back to sleep with all of the commotion around him, so he lifted his head up again and saw now his body tied down to the bed.

"Don't worry, this is so you remain stable. We didn't know if you have any broken bones," said the coastguard with the helmet.

"I'm alright, I'm alright. Just please, untie me," Darien said finally breaking his silence.

He could feel every cell in his body and knew nothing was broken. The coastguards gladly obliged, uncorking the bands across his chest, legs and shoulders. He sat up straight on the bed and looked at his best friend who was still shaken up by everything that had occurred.

"I think I've ruined your big day, chief," said Darien as he laid his hand on Samer's tense shoulder.

Samer burst into anxious laughter. "You are insane man," replied Samer as he rubbed his neck.

Seeing Samer fidget and speak in his high voice, Darien could not help but remember Kafka. He smiled with melancholy at his friend and said, "What happened?"

"I should ask you that," replied Samer.

Darien proceeded with patience, telling Samer how he had met Nadia at the deck and decided to impress her by jumping in the water.

Samer told him that his story matched Nadia's, as she had already told Samer and the rest of the crew on the boat. She had only missed the bit explaining that Darien's foolish act was done to impress her. "Well, after you jumped, Nadia came running to me and Aisha. We were shit scared, Bro," he said as his eyes opened wide. "We informed the captain and he immediately dispatched the Abu Dhabi coastguard. You're lucky because it didn't take them more than eight minutes to show up. A full rescue mission rolled out. The place was like a scene in a movie. Speedboats, rafts and a couple of helicopters, including the one you're in now."

Darien remained quiet. "You were gone for a while, almost an hour. You were passed out when we found you. All I can say is you're real lucky. If it wasn't for the sparkly glitter on your clothes, we wouldn't have spotted you in the dark!" he laughed. "So tell me who did you get to grinding with on the boat? Definitely couldn't have been Nadia, 'cause I know she's not the type to get all up close and personal with a guy she just met. So who was it, you cheeky bastard?"

"What do you mean sparkly glitter?" Darien had no idea what Samer was talking about.

"Ah, come on! Don't play dumb, man! Who was it?" said Samer as he brushed the sleeve on Darien's tuxedo, causing little golden particles to disperse around them.

Darien's spine stiffened, his muscles tightened and his eyes opened up wide. He looked down and saw Rumla glued all over his clothes. It hadn't been a dream.

"Whoa, you look like you've just seen a djinn!" said Samer as he pulled his weight back on his chair.

"How long was I gone for?" Darien frantically asked.

"I don't know, about three hours or so," replied Samer.

"Three hours and fourteen minutes to be precise. That's when we spotted you in the water," jumped in one of the coastguards. "This is the first time we have found someone this quickly at night."

"I don't know how to thank you gentlemen," said Darien. He had been right all along. There was good in this world.

"Yeah, well except for the few serious cuts you have on your neck, you were just fine when we found you," chimed in Samer.

Darien reached for his neck and felt the marks Hubal had left on his skin. "I don't know what to say Sam, thank you, thank you for coming back for me."

"Hey man, I was just doing what's right. I know you would do the same. Besides it would have been a major travesty if you had died on my wedding day. Don't think I could have lived with that," replied Samer.

If only Darien could tell his best friend what he had just been through. The real travesty would have been if he weren't to have found himself sitting in this helicopter. There would have been no tomorrow for Samer to live for.

"You are really fortunate," said one of the coastguards.

"*Alhamdulillah* I am," replied Darien as he looked out the window onto the beautiful world they were all blessed with.

"Sam, I don't know what to say, I can't say sorry enough for ruining your big day."

"Are you insane? Don't worry about it. Just don't ruin my next three!" Samer let out a loud laugh as he always did when he cracked a joke. "Great, well listen it was too late to call your mum and sister so they have no idea how memorable my wedding has turned out to be. Now your vitals are all fine but you definitely need some rest. And I need to get back to a freaked out wife."

"I'm going to have to make it up to Aisha," said a worried Darien. He knew next to wanting to be princesses, women dreamed of this day from a young age.

"Yes, you do. And you can do that by taking Nadia out for dinner so that I can have some quality time with my wife." Samer was so glad to see his friend that he just couldn't stop joking around. "Well look, you need to rest. So our brothers here have been generous enough to book you in the Emirates Palace for as long as you need. We're just all so glad you are still alive."

"Wow, that's very kind of you all," said Darien. This was the Middle Eastern benevolence he had grown up with as a child. The Emirati hospitality in particular was as warm as the weather in which it resided. "But I would like to go home if that is okay with you all."

"Are you sure? It is not a problem from our end, we can take you to Dubai right now," said one of the coastguards.

"I would be grateful if you could, yes," replied Darien.

He did not want to milk their extended courtesy. Just the mere fact that they had come for him was more than he could ask for. The coastguard then spoke through his microphone and the helicopter changed directions and headed towards Dubai. He was about to use the helipad made out of recycled concrete at Orchard Tower for the very first time.

"Alright *shabab*," said the pilot—*shabab* being an Arabic phrase meaning youth. "Sit tight, we will be there in no time."

Darien was in no rush. He sat back, closed his eyes and dreamed of being back on Ashkhas Island.

Chapter 28
A Soul Rises at Dawn

It was not long before the helicopter reached the top of Orchard Tower. Without his Rolex, Darien could not tell how much time had passed exactly. When they arrived, he shook the hands of the men who saved him and hugged his friend goodbye. He hopped out of the helicopter and in towards his building. Samer sensed a change in Darien. He was not his regular morbid self nor was he the ebullient Darien he knew growing up. There was something peculiarly calm about Darien. Samer could only sum up his friend's demeanor a result of a near death experience. He was to go on his honeymoon and give his friend some time to get his marbles back.

Darien got to the entrance of his apartment. The moment he jumped into the water, he had left his wallet, keys and cell phone out on the boat. He had retrieved them from the coastguard, but had yet to read the messages and see the missed calls on his phone. When he entered his apartment he went right towards the window, where it was still the break of dawn. The sun would soon wake everybody up. Turning to face his untidy flat, the piled up dishes behind his kitchen counter, the wires dangling around his television and the grey sofa pillows with imprints of trees each reminded him of the woodlands of Ashkhas Island. There was a deafening silence in his room. The only sound he heard was that of his own heartbeat matching the sound of the city's quiet pulse.

The citizens of Dubai Marina were yet to get up today in search of what had brought them to this enchanted city. But in this apartment, on one corner of an entire floor, the life of one twenty-six-year-old had entirely changed.

He had found riches beyond worldly imagination. He had found the never ending well of love. He had found faith on a spellbound island with the help of creatures he will never see roam this world again.

Most important of all, he had found himself. One thing he could not get his head around was how he had discovered himself only when the exploits of evil had revealed themselves. Why was it that a gape of light entered his heart in the lurking dark shadow pits of Hubal's chamber? Hope had only revealed herself to him when he was immersed in darkness. He realized that if it had not been for the malice he had walked through, he would not have been enlightened.

He made his way to his bathroom. He could use a shower. He threw his dried clothes on the floor only to retract his steps—this was a new Darien, after all—picking up his clothes and throwing them in his laundry basket.

His mind was adrift. He was not thinking about his career, family or even father, his ex-fiancé or former boss who had tried vigorously to clip his wings and spirit. The only things on his mind were the last parting words of Evren and Hubal. He was so entrenched in the moment that he had failed to pay attention to even the black little dots that followed his eyesight now for more than thirteen years.

Looking at the laundry basket, he saw the glittering Rumla floating and dancing around the borders of his steel basket. For a moment, he thought of grabbing a bottle and filling it with some of the remaining Rumla as a tribute to his adventures on Ashkhas Island. He knew though that the magical sand didn't belong in an urn. It belonged on the island and nowhere else.

He walked into the bathroom and stood right in front of the mirror.

He leaned over the sink as his shoulders shifted forward as he looked at his own reflection. He cast his eyes down and for the first time, he could see himself clearly. His glare was fixed to the eyes looking back at him. He began to take deep breaths as he observed the cuts that had dried on his neck, heaving in more air than his lungs could take. The marks showed how deep Hubal had dug his nails into Darien's neck.

He raised his hand just to feel the scabs forming on his skin. Then he saw a patch of Rumla stuck on his forearm through the mirror in front of him. He ran the tap water, held his hand under it, and started to wash off the Rumla. Rays of light began to slide under the crack of his bathroom door. The water ran, and its flowing melodies synced in perfect harmony with the scorch of the shambling sun.

He held his hand under it and started to scrub the golden Rumla on his forearm away.

It didn't come off. Darien's eyes glowed with surprise. He reached for the scrub hanging by his bathtub and scrubbed his hand a little harder, yet the golden dust stayed bound to the surface of his skin. He scrubbed harder and harder as his skin exfoliated, revealing a sunlit golden texture. He scrubbed as hard as he could. The skin around his whole arm, wrist, palm and fingers began to peel away with each rub.

When he raised his hand, it was covered in gold from the elbow to the tip of his fingers. The creeping rays of the sun reflected radiantly against his mesmerizing aurum-glazed hand. He raised his golden plaque and gazed at it through the mirror.

He glanced right back at the man staring at him through the Ayna. He heaved three deep breaths. He looked right at himself and took in even deeper breaths. Darien realized that he was finally home.

He had arrived.

Exhale.